# THE GOLDEN SEAL

## NINJANS 3

Dave Kwan

# DISCLAIMER

This book is a work of Fiction.
Names, characters, businesses,
places, events, locales, and
incidents are either the products
of the author's imagination
or used in a fictitious manner.
Any resemblance to actual persons,
living or dead, or actual events
is purely coincidental.

Book Cover Credit: Artwork by Travel mania - Adobe Stock

File#: 367909367  JPEG  6016 x 3573px

# DEDICATION

This book is dedicated
to my three grown children.
Each of whom have their own
personality, skills and talents.
It's my wish to say in print,
I'm very proud of you!

# CHAPTER ONE

*The Bus To Venture*

A Greyhound zooms along the ribbon of black tarmac in the hot desert. The Highway meanders around rugged hills and snakes between towering rock canyons, until it opens up to long empty stretches of pavement. Inside the air-conditioned bus, the passengers read novels, recline to snooze, or simply gaze out at the sage brush and cactus that dot the passing terrain. This is 'Big Sky' country with vast stretches of unoccupied land that has little sign of people or habitat. This sun-baked landscape belongs to the desert creatures of the region - the coyote, hawk, rattlesnake, cougar, and eagle. The only sign  of human activity are the trucks, cars and buses that ply the highway, moving their way from town to town, and city to city. After considerable time, the Greyhound turns off the Highway onto a tarmac road, and motors past the large wood sign that reads American Indian Reservation of Venture. The bus goes past stores, homes, a Post Office, a Police Station, Community Hall, and a Baseball Diamond. The bus tires kick up a small trail of dust that covers the paved roadway. Inside the bus, passengers are a mixed bag of travellers - locals, visiting relatives, seniors, folks with city jobs, and High School and College kids. The students are either on their cell phones, slouch in their seats, or just stare out the window. The man driving the bus steers the vehicle toward the four-way stop with the flashing red light, slows the engine down and presses the brakes - this is the Venture's 'Town Centre'. The driver announces, "Last stop, Venture - everyone out!" The people get up to line the aisle to  leave the bus. In the middle of the passengers is Jody Long Grass, a tall attractive athletic gal in her early 20's with long shiny black hair. As Jody reaches the steps to exit, she turns to the bus driver and comments, "I just finished College so I won't be riding with you anymore. Just wanted to say Thanks!" The driver lifts his cap visor for better eye contact, smiles and replies, "It's been a pleasure Jody! Wish more kids were like you - polite and respectful." Jody gives a parting smile, turns and descends the steps to the dusty ground outside. She hoists her backpack and looks around and spots the red pickup truck parked across the road and waves. Karen Long Grass, her good looking middle-aged Caucasian mom gives a wave and beckons from the open truck window, "Hurry Jody! - Or you'll be late." Jody quickly glances for traffic then scoots across the road. She tosses her backpack into the cargo box, climbs in the passenger seat to buckle up, then asks, "Is Grandpa at the house yet?" Her mom looks at her daughter and remarks, "He's so excited - he arrived two hours early. We don't want to keep your Grandpa waiting!" Karen starts the pickup and pulls onto the road as Jody puts down her window. As the truck moves along, Jody's hair dances in the breeze. Jody looks at her mom and grins, "I've been waiting for this all day!" Her mom glances at her and remarks, "All I know is he booked a fancy city restaurant — said he wants your Grad Dinner to be special! Just the two of you - A grandpa and his granddaughter!" The red pickup motors down the reservation road and Karen turns onto a Concession, the road sign reads - PLAINS ROAD. The truck goes over a couple hills, around some bends and down a straight stretch, until the pickup approaches a roadside mail box with large letters - LONG GRASS. Karen signals and turns into the driveway and cuts the engine. The mother and daughter quickly get out.

Inside the raised brick bungalow, Carl Long Grass, Jody's grandfather, is a tall fit elderly man with long braided white hair and a friendly face. He looks out the big front window and gets excited and yells out, "She's here! Brian - she's here!" Brian Long Grass, Karen's Native American husband and Jody's dad, comes out of the kitchen. Brian is handsome and muscular with salt and pepper hair that reaches his shoulders. Brian walks over to Carl, pats the old man's back and hands him the car keys and comments, "Your car's gassed up - all set!" At that moment the front door opens and Karen and Jody walk in. Carl breaks into a big smile as Jody rushes over with a hug. Carl gazes fondly at his granddaughter and remarks, "Are you ready for our fancy dinner?" Jody steps over and puts her backpack in an armchair and replies, "Been excited all day, Grandpa! I've never been inside a high class restaurant before1" Karen slips alongside to playfully squeeze Jody's shoulder and comments, "I'm sure you'll be the first girl on the Reserve to dine at a Three Star French restaurant!" Jody gives her mom a big grin. Brain speaks up, "We'd better let them go - it's a 90 minute drive to city, considering traffic - they should head out now." Carl walks to the front entry and takes his embroidered tan buckskin jacket off the coat rack, and turns to the trio and remarks, "As soon as she can change clothes and pretty up - we're outta here!" Jody beams a big smile and dashes to her bedroom and closes the door. There's the sound of rummaging with drawers opening and closing, Carl and Jody's parents exchange glances and grin. Suddenly, the handle clicks and the bedroom door opens to reveal Jody standing there in black dress slacks with a stylish red top and wearing a sparkling necklace with matching earrings. Karen, Brian and Carl are mesmerized. Brian with a faltering voice utters, "Is that my little girl all grown up?" Jody steps into the living room looking classy and chic. Karen comes over with a loving hug and remarks, "Honey, you look so pretty!" Jody smiles at her mom's words. As Brian and Karen step aside, Carl walks over and drapes an ivory shawl over Jody's shoulders, he smiles and comments, "This is what all the fashionable gals are wearing in Europe these days." Jody goes to stand in front of the full length mirror and twirls around and admires the new wardrobe addition, "Grandpa, it's beautiful! - I love it!" Carl looks at the parents, "We should be back by 10:00 pm." As the grandfather and granddaughter move toward the front door, Karen quickly blocks them and exclaims, "Almost forget - we need pictures! After all, this is an important occasion!" Brian and Karen hold ups their cell phones to snap photos. Jody is a little embarrassed and remarks, Mom! Dad! Please!" The parents put away their phones. Carl turns and opens the front door and gestures to Jody with a polite line, "Ladies first!" Jody grins and replies, "Why such a gentleman!" As Jody steps through the doorway, Carl turns to Brain and Karen and remarks, "Only the best for my precious granddaughter!", then he shuts the door. Karen and Brian move to the large picture window and stare out as they watch Carl and Jody get into the car. Brian sighs and breaks the silence, "As soon as Jody got in her first year at College, he's been planning this big celebration. Now, he finally gets to show Jody off." The couple watch as the car pulls out of the driveway and heads down the road out of sight.

# CHAPTER TWO
*The College Grad Celebration*

The Three Star gourmet establishment has richly upholstered wing chairs at tables with fine linen cloths, classy lamps, candles, and a lovely flower centrepiece. The restaurant interior is decorated with French paintings, sculptures, and large vases with beautiful flowers. The Maitre D has a jacket with tails and all the servers wear white gloves. In a small cove at the side, a string quartet sit on a raised platform and play classical music. On the sidewalk outside, Carl and Jody approach the restaurant entrance, and Carl opens the polished brass doors with bevelled glass, and they enter. As they stand inside the stately foyer, the Maitre D looks up from his podium with its tiny light and bids welcome, "Good evening! Do you have a reservation?" Carl steps toward the Maitre D and politely announces, "A booking for two - the name is Long Grass." The Maitre D scans the list, smiles and remarks, "Voila! I see your reservation. Please follow me to your table." The Maitre D promptly leads Carl and Jody to a table for two nestled along the decorative interior wall. Carl gets seated as the Maitre D pulls out a chair for the young lady. Once Jody is seated, the Maitre D smiles, turns and walks back to his podium in the reception area. Within seconds, two servers with white gloves attend, one gives Carl and Jody a Menu then stands ready with pen and order pad. The other server pours water into the two stylish crystal drinking glasses, then quickly leaves. Carl and Jody read over the Menu. Jody lifts her head to watch the string quartet play the lovely music of Mozart. She turns and looks at the Menu - then flips it over to see the back is blank! Jody leans forward and whispers, "Grandpa. There's no prices!" The grandfather smiles, looks at the server, who politely smiles, then resumes his order taking pose. Carl replies, "High class dining restaurants do not show prices." Jody's eyes widen as she responds,

"How will people know the cost?" Carl looks at Jody and explains, "When you dine at a place like this - you come prepared to spend a lot of money! Don't worry everything's okay! Remember, this is my Graduation treat!" At this moment, the server turns to look at the Maitre D who gives a puzzled look; the server tilts his head, shrugs his shoulders, then faces the table and asks, "Are you ready to order? - What will the Mademoiselle be having?" Carl gives Jody a reassuring look and smiles. Jody scans the Menu and remarks, "The Roast Chicken sounds nice." The server jots her order, then he casts a glance at Carl, who informs, "For starters - we will have the Steak Tartar, Salade de Maison and the Crispy Escargot." The server smiles widely as he writes, "And for your Main - Monsieur?" Carl replies, "I'll have the Duck Confit." The server gives an ever so slight nod and comments, "Excellent choice! The server asks, "And your choice of wine - Monsieur?" Carl lifts eyes and replies, "We will not be ordering wine tonight." The Server politely nods, smiles, takes both Menus and comments, "Please enjoy your meal." As the man promptly leaves to disappear into the far kitchen, another server approaches, lights the table candle, then quickly withdraws. Jody looks around at the restaurant's beautiful decor, and listens to the classical music as she basks in the glow of the candlelight, and exclaims, "This so wonderful, Grandpa! I feel special being here." Carl reaches out his arm to clasp his granddaughter's hand, and tenderly remarks, "You are special, Jody! Special from the first day you were born. You deserve a night out like this (Carl's eyes get moist) At my age, I might not get another opportunity to celebrate my granddaughter's accomplishments!" Jody looks at her grandpa and replies, "I've learned so much from you, Grandpa! It was you who trained me - taught me everything I know." As Jody fondly gazes at her grandpa, she remembers the time when being very young, she and Carl rehearsed Martial Arts Katas. She recalls how Carl taught her to punch, block, spin and kick. Jody reflects on how they practiced Sticky Hands, and how Carl taught her to throw the Shuriken, the sharp metal stars sinking deep into the wood targets. As the candlelight flickers, she thinks of the times when she and her grandfather sparred with wood Katana swords, and how they both sat in deep meditation. As other patrons get seated at tables nearby, Jody comes out of her inner reflection. Carl smiles at Jody and remarks, "I tried to teach you everything I know - hoping you'd go further and become even better." By now the server brings the Appetizers to their table. Jody gives the Tartar an odd look and pokes it with her fork and asks, "What's this?" Carl chuckles and replies, "Raw meat! It's delicious." As they dine, the restaurant gradually gets filled with patrons at tables. Jody and Grandpa Carl heartily enjoy their fine French cuisine. Jody savours the Roast Chicken and Carl feasts on the Duck Confit. When they finish their plates, a server pours them more water and politely removes their dishes. Jody dabs the linen napkin to her lips and remarks, "Grandpa, that was wonderful! - I've never tasted such nice food!" Carl replies with a twinkle in his eye, "I'm so happy you're enjoying this!" The attending server approaches the table and asks, "Monsieur, Mademoiselle - will you be having desert?" Carl looks at Jody and winks his eye and responds, "Are the deserts good?" The server lifts his eye brow in alarm and quickly replies, "Monsieur! The House of Andrea has the best deserts in the city!" Jody gives a slight giggle and Carl remarks, "In that case, please bring us the Opera Cake and the Poire Belle Helene." The server smiles and replies, "Your selection is superb! Merci!" As the server leaves the table, Jody playfully tilts her head at Carl and asks, "When did you know so much about French stuff?" The grandfather sits back in his upholstered dining chair and straightens his long white braids and comments, "When you've been around as long as I have - you pick up a thing or two - like French cuisine." Jody grins and can't resist asking, "What other stuff do you know?" Carl gazes at Jody and replies, "Over the years, I've learned some Spanish, French - and even some Japanese. (Pause) I've studied Japan for twenty years. The country has a fascinating culture. Actually, I'm planning a special trip there after the summer." Jody quips, "Special trip? - What makes it so special?" Carl looks pensively at his granddaughter and remarks, "There's unfinished business I must take care of. Something that's waited far too long!" At that second, the server brings the deserts and sets them down. Jody stares at the Opera Cake and the appealing Pear and Cream desert. Carl divides the two deserts and gives Jody a portion of each. Jody digs her fork into the Opera Cake and takes a bite, and her eyes open wide with culinary delight!

# CHAPTER THREE
## *Trouble Downtown*

Night is upon the city, and light from building windows and the glow of the street lamps create a warm atmosphere downtown. The restaurant's posh entrance doors open and Carl and Jody step out onto the sidewalk, exiting the fine dining establishment. Jody wraps the shawl over her shoulders to fend off the cool air of the evening. The grandfather and granddaughter hold hands and begin to leisurely stroll past trendy shops and interesting boutiques. Jody looks over and comments, "Thanks Grandpa! I'm so happy you took me here." Carl replies with an endearing smile, "I wanted you to taste gourmet food and enjoy a high class setting." They walk along and Jody stops to admire an outfit in the Boutique window. She remarks, "This place is so different from the Reserve. Everything is so new and shiny — so nice!" Carl bends his head slightly as he gazes at Jody and comments, "Life isn't always about what's on the outside. - What's on the inside is much more important!" Jody turns to chime, "The City seems to have it all - everything's here!" Carl replies in a voice schooled with wisdom and experience, "Our Reserve doesn't have all this fancy stuff! What we do have is very valuable! - Our people are linked to American History, and our Tribal roots go deep into the very earth." Jody reaches out to clasp her grandfather's hand, "That's why I love you so much, Grandpa! - You're so smart and so wise!" Carl playfully squeezes Jody's hand and replies in jest, "And really really old!" They both laugh as they walk the sidewalk and turn the corner. Carl and Jody stop as they see barricades with flashing amber lights across the street midway up their route. Maintenance crews are working to repair the sidewalk and repave the road surface. Jody exclaims, "What will we do?" Carl scans about and points to a side alley and comments, "I believe this alley will take us the next street over to the car." The grandfather and granddaughter turn from the sidewalk and proceed into the dark corridor.

The passageway has spotty lighting that only illuminates certain spots as the alley zigzags its way behind the large brick buildings. Carl holds Jody's hand as they go through the passageway. They turn a corner and enter one of the alley's open areas. Suddenly, they stumble upon a street gang with a drug deal gone wrong. A dead body lays on the ground in a pool of blood. The gangsters are shocked and rivet their attention. Carl braces and puts his arm out to protect Jody. The gang's big leader yells, "Witnesses! We don't want witnesses. Get 'em!" The street gang swiftly spread out to surround on all sides. Carl keeps his guard and swiftly eyes Jody and remarks, "Twin Tigers - like we practiced!" Jody nods and takes a battle stance and replies, "Back to back - Repeal attack!" Carl and Jody quickly position back to back. Grandfather and granddaughter get into battle stance for the pending assault. Jody's shawl falls to the ground. The gangsters pace back and forth and flash their knives and clubs to intimidate. A gangster threatens, "You're dead meat old man! (Leers) But that young thing with you (Laughs) We'll show her a real good time!" All the gangsters start to Trash Talk! Carl scans the circle of thugs and whispers a Ninjan adage, "Eagles fly above the storm!" The gang of thugs block escape as the gang leader stands in front of Carl. The hoodlums threaten from all sides, and the leader steps out to stare down Carl. Carl boldly holds his ground and doesn't flinch, Jody keeps her eyes on the gangsters confronting her. The gang leader sneers and remarks, "He's just an old mangy Indian. Home Boy - take Him out!" A big thug steps out from the pack to size up Carl, then the brute raises his big arm and strides forward. The thug swings his fist - Carl grabs and torques his wrist to buckle the brute to the pavement. Carl boots the him away. Carl looks at the gang and emphasizes, "We don't want trouble! Just let us go." Big Home Boy gets up in a rage and lunges. Carl spear-thrusts his fingers into the nap of the thug's neck. The gangster collapses to the pavement, contorts and gasps for breath. All the gangsters are stunned their big guy got dropped! Their leader yells, "Rip him to shreds! - Kill him!" Gangsters around Carl and Jody begin to flip and twirl butterfly knives. They attack! One thug wildly swipes his blade. Carl blocks and grabs his arm to snap and dislocate the guy's shoulder. The gangster drops in agony. One tough repeatedly jabs his knife at Jody's torso. She kicks the blade away and releases a roundhouse to knock him out! Two gangsters lunge at Jody and she spins to block and flip one hard to the ground. The other thug grabs and squeezes Jody tight. She gives him a forceful head butt and gets released, then she strikes his vulnerable areas to disable him. The thug falls over. From the side, one gangster swings mightily at Carl with a metal rebar. Carl dodges, then grabs and bends his wrist to buckle him down. Carl belts the guy unconscious. As Carl is turned sideways, three homies with clubs rush from the front. Jody calls out in alarm, "Grandpa! Look out!" The three thugs spread out and violently swing and swipe their clubs. Carl bobs and ducks to avoid hits. He blocks, grabs a club from one thug and knocks him out! Carl takes the club to block the other two attackers. One thug runs at him and Carl pummels the attacker in a flurry of blows. The thug caves. The other thug swings and Carl flips the third thug to land hard yards away. Carl quickly turns to check on Jody. She's worried! Carl is exhausted, sweaty, and catches his breath. The gang leader bellows, "He's done! Finish him off!" Jody cries out, "Leave him alone! He's 83 years old." A street thug exclaims, "What a tough old geezer!" The street gang break out laughing - then, they get dead serious. Carl leans his hand on Jody's shoulder to steady himself. Jody looks into his eyes - Carl shakes his head! The gangsters close in. Suddenly, Carl clutches his chest, his face in excruciating anguish - he collapses unconscious! Jody cries out, "Grandpa! Grandpa!" A gangster yells loudly, "Hey! The old man got a heart attack!" The gangsters start to edge forward as Jody is bent over her Grandpa. She lifts her head - there's fire in her eyes! Jody springs from her crouch, spins to kick two nearby thugs unconscious! She quickly pivots to drive her fist into a thug's throat, then, pokes her fingers into another's eyes. He screams! The street gang leaders yells, "She's just a girl! Show her who's boss!" Jody rivets her eyes to the leader and harshly remarks, "You beat up an old man - now try someone younger!" The remaining street thugs brandish their switchblades, knives and clubs to attack her. One thug stretches his arms to grab her, she zips between his legs and drives her foot into his 'family jewels'. The guy buckles over in pain! She flips upright to explode a roundhouse to knock out another thug. A homie to her side slashes his blade at her. She blocks his swing and wrenches his arm to dislocate his shoulder. Now, only the street gang leader and a lieutenant are still standing. As Jody strides toward them, the leader shoves the other guy forward. He forcefully swings his fist, Jody ducks each punch. She strikes him with a torrent of blows - it's light out! The leader stands there alone. He flips and twirls his butterfly knife with bravado and teases, "Just you and me, little girlie! Let's see how good you really are?" The gang leader swipes his blade at Jody's face. She ducks. He repeatedly jabs and Jody dodges each lunge. One blade thrust goes close by her face and cuts off some of her locks of hair. The thug boss swipes hard and cuts Jody's forearm, she grabs the wound - blood seeps down to her hand. Jody looks into the hoodlum's eyes with gritty resolve, "You picked the wrong Indians to mess with!" The thug lunges with all his might. Jody sidesteps, grabs his arm and wrenches the knife loose. She drives her knee into his face, then gives him a powerful double kick. The gangster drops to the pavement - knocked out! Around her, gangsters wither in pain, incapacitated, while others remain unconscious. Jody takes out her cell phone and quickly dials 911. The Emergency Operator announces, "Hello 911! What is your emergency?" Jody replies, "My Grandpa had a heart attack! Please hurry! Quick!" The Operator asks, "What is your location?" Jody swiftly scans about and replies, "Some crooked alley near a French Restaurant - workers are paving the street!" The Operator informs, "Please keep calm! Stay with your Grandfather. Help is on the way." Jody pockets her phone as she leans over Carl. She gently touches his face. Soon, the sound of Police and Ambulance sirens approach.

# CHAPTER FOUR

*Hospital Emergency*

Carl lays unconscious in an Intensive Care Unit bed. Hospital tubes and electronic leads connect his body to monitors and medical equipment. The steady electronic sounds of medical devices fill the room - Beep! Beep! Beep! Jody sits in a bedside chair and keeps vigil over her Grandpa. A nurse enters the room to check the leads, tubes - reads the monitors and medical equipment - then leaves. Seconds later, Brian and Karen appear in the doorway. They rush to Carl's side, their eyes trace the old man's motionless form. Brian looks at Jody with concern, "What happened?" Jody stands up, clasps her Grandpa's hand near the bed railing and replies, "We left the restaurant and walked to the car. The street was blocked so we took an alley - that's when we ran into the street gang." Karen utters in alarm, "Street Gang! Oh Jody!" Mom comes over to put an arm around her daughter. Jody looks at her parents and remarks, "Grandpa fought them real good - took down several until the heart attack. - I took out the rest (Pause) The Police arrested them all!" Brian scans the monitors and medical machines, and exchanges glances with Karen. He holds Carl's hand and comments, "He looks so weak and fragile - nothing like the Ninjan Master he is!" Brain has a Flashback to when as a teenager, Carl trained him with Ninjan swords. At that moment, the nurse enters the room, comes up to inspect the solution and check the IV needle in Carl's arm. She glances at the trio and gives an assuring smile. And comments, "The doctors will be in shortly to give an update." The nurse jots something on the bed chart and leaves the room. A few minutes later, two physicians wearing white coats, one young and the other older, walk into the room and approach the small family. The older doctor smiles and greets them, "Hello! I'm Dr. Churchill (points) and this is Dr. Swartz." Brian extends his hand to greet and comments, "Hi! I'm

Brian (gestures) this is my wife Karen and our daughter Jody." The two doctors go beside the bed to inspect Carl and to check the monitors and bed chart. Dr. Churchill looks at the family and remarks, "We want to run tests right away - lab work, X-rays, and a MRI. (Inspects Carl's chest) The surgery went well, but we just want to be sure everything is okay!" Karen looks at Brian and asks the seasoned doctor, "How long before you find out?" Dr. Swartz looks at the trio, smiles and replies, "The tests won't take long - we should know in a day or two." Brian pulls Karen to his side and nods acknowledgement. The two doctors bid bye and exit the room and turn the corner down the hall. Jody glances at her dad, "Is Grandpa going to be all right?" Brian gives her a reassuring squeeze, then glances at Carl and remarks, "Your Grandpa's a tough hombre! I'm sure he'll be okay." Over the next couple of days, Radiology Technicians position Carl for X-rays, a nurse withdraws blood from Carl's forearm, Medical Technicians work on Lab samples, and Carl lays on a flat table nestled in an enormous MRI machine. Finally, a team of doctors examine the MRI, X-rays and Lab Reports.

Carl is awake and sits upright in his inclined hospital bed. He has an IV tube and a couple leads attached. A monitor stands on each side like two electronic sentinels. Brian and Karen sit in the upholstered visitor chairs, while Jody stands beside Carl hovering like a Guardian Angel. The sounds of the Hospital Intercom system echoes into the room - "Paging IV Nurse. Paging IV Nurse." At that moment, Doctors Churchill and Swartz and another doctor, all in white coats, walk into the room and approach the family. The physicians nod a greeting to everyone. Dr. Churchill holds a folder with X-rays, Lab Reports and Charts. The doctors exchange glances and Dr. Churchill clears his throat and speaks, "We've examined the X-rays, Lab results and the MRI. (Pause) I'm afraid we have bad news!" Brain, Karen and Jody perk up at Dr. Churchill's announcement. Carl lays in his bed quiet. Brian looks at the doctor with grey hair and asks, "What is it Doctor?" The senior physician casts his eyes on Carl, then looks at the other three, and replies, "The Stint Surgery went well and Carl's heart is stable and in recovery. - However, the MRI, X-rays and Lab Reports tell us that Carl has Cancer - Stage Four Lymphoma!" Brian's face turns white. Karen gasps aloud! Jody begins to cry and turns to hug her Grandpa. Carl is calm and serene. Jody looks into her Grandpa's eyes and remarks, "You'll be okay Grandpa? You're going to fight this!

Right?" Brian looks at the doctors, "Is there anything you can do? Radiation? Treatments? Chemo?" Dr. Churchill replies with tender diplomacy, "I'm sorry! There's little we can do when Lymphoma is this advanced." The elderly doctor steps up beside his patient, and Carl looks directly into the doctor's eyes and asks, "It's okay Doc! Just tell me how long I have?" The grey haired doctor looks at the family, then glances at Carl and replies, "Four months! You have four months before the Cancer takes over. (Pats Carl's arm) I'm sorry! (Pause) We've made arrangements for you to be moved to Palliative Care - that will make things easier for you." Carl looks at Dr. Churchill and remarks, "Doc. I've made peace with my Creator long time ago." Jody sobs, "Oh Grandpa!" Carl lifts his eyes toward Brian, Karen and Jody and comments, "I'm not afraid to die! - It's just hard to leave your loved ones behind!" The senior Doctor steps away from the bedside, and the three doctors tactfully withdraw to exit. Brain, Karen and Jody come beside Carl to comfort him with their support, hugs and tears.

Two weeks later...

The Palliative Care Wing has a residential touch. The furniture, vases of flowers, wall pictures and room decor, create an atmosphere similar to being at home. The Doctors, nurses and staff, do their best to help patients during their final days. Carl has lost muscle mass and looks thin and weak. His shoulder bones protrude, his once muscular arms are skinny, and his face is slightly drawn-in. When thirsty, he sips water through a straw and cup.

# CHAPTER FIVE
*Carl's Dying Request*

Knock! Knock!

Carl lifts his eyes to the doorway to see Jody, Karen and Brian enter his room with loving smiles. Jody holds a fresh bouquet of flowers. She walks to the window ledge and places the arrangement near the Get Well cards and other flowers. Jody comments with a cheery smile, "Here Grandpa - these will help brighten your day!" Brian and Karen lean in to greet and hug Carl. Jody moves beside her Grandpa to reach out and hold his hand. Carl gazes at the trio and remarks, "Aren't you guys tired of visiting me? - Must interfere with other things you have to do!" Brian and Karen exchange eye contact and Brian replies, "What we need to do - is be with you! We love you!" Carl tears up and Jody leans in with an affectionate hug. Karen looks at Carl and comments, "We have things covered. Please don't worry about us." Jody looks into her Grandpa's eyes and speaks sweetly, "I don't want to be anywhere else but right here with you!"

Carl scans his eyes from Brian to Karen to Jody. He clears his throat and reaches for another sip of water. Jody grabs the cup and brings it near to make it easier for Carl to sip. Carl remarks, "Thanks Jody! - This medication dries out my throat. Ahem! (Pause) Brian, I need you to do something." Brian moves closer to stand beside Carl and responds, "Anything! Whatever you need!" Carl turns his face toward Jody, then looks at Brian and remarks, "Inside the black armoire, underneath my Ninjan robe - there's a black leather pouch that hangs on a hook. Please bring it to me." Brian nods and replies, "Don't worry! I'll get it for you." Carl gives a weak nod. Jody reaches to gently glide her fingers on the side of his white braid. Carl coughs and begins to close his eyes and quickly falls asleep. Karen watches Carl and comments with sadness, "He gets weaker each day!" Karen comes over to hug Brain for solace. Jody stands transfixed - she scans Carl's emancipated body and her eyes well up with tears.

Carl's house is a small white wood cottage with some green ivy that climbs one side. The cottage sits nestled amid lovely pine trees and faces a forest stream. Brian enters the home and goes into Carl's bedroom and stands before the big black armoire. He reaches out and opens the double doors. Brian's eyes glance at the interior filled with Ninjan weapons and clothing. He scans the black weapons - the Ninjato and Katana swords, war club, Tomahawk, battle Sickle, Knives, Shuriken metal stars, and black bow and quiver of black arrows. Brian stretches his arm inside and moves the black robe aside and sees the black pouch hanging on a hook. He grabs the black drawstring and lifts the leather pouch away. Brian closes the armoire, turns and leaves the bedroom and exits the small white cottage toward his car.

At the Palliative Care Unit, a nurse helps Carl with his meal as he reclines in bed at an upright angle. His arms are unable to manage the feeding task. The nurse spoon feeds him the last of the green peas and carrots. Carl slowly chews and swallows, then the nurse gives him a sip of water. Finished the meal, the nurse removes the food tray and heads toward the door. She greets Brian, Karen and Jody as they enter. Carl sees his family and manages a smile. He becomes energized at their presence and life comes into his eyes. Karen, Brian and Jody greet Carl with loving hugs, kisses, and hand touches of support. Brian raises the black leather pouch for Carl to see and remarks, "Brought the pouch as you requested!" Brian places the pouch in Carl's palm. The old man smiles deeply and looks at all three and comments, "Thank you very much! This pouch contains something very special!" He shifts his gaze to Jody and moves his finger to beckon her, and remarks, "Jody! Please open the pouch and take out what's inside." Jody nods, picks up the pouch and pulls the drawstring open. She reaches in her fingers with child-like wonder and remarks, "It feels heavy - maybe a stone?" Everyone's eyes are focused with intensity. She pulls out her hand and opens it. A shiny gold square pillar about 5 inches high lays in her palm, the object has strange engravings and peculiar indentations on all four sides. Jody holds it up for display to

Brain and Karen. Brian comes close and Jody deposits the square gold pillar into is hand. He closely examines it and feels its weight and turns it over a few times, and remarks, "Whatever it is - it's solid gold! Must be really expensive and worth lots of money!" Karen comes beside to see for herself. She handles the gold column, then gives it back to Jody. Jody lifts the pillar up for closer inspection and glides her fingers tips over the details. Her eyes zero in on the engravings, design, and indentations. Carl smiles at her and extends his arm with an open palm. Jody goes beside him and lays the gold object in his weathered hand, and comments,"Grandpa - what is it?" Carl gazes at the square gold column and remarks, "This is the Golden Seal! It's the key to a secret Ninja Treasure! (Pause) It's been passed down generation to generation." Brain, Karen and Jody exchange looks of surprise and awe. Carl lifts his eyes toward them and continues, "The Ninja Sword Master Katsu gave it to his son, Takeshi. The Ninja Master Takeshi passed the Golden Seal to his Shoshone Apprentice and adopted son, Yuji. Yuji granted it to his son, Kamatsu; who gave it to his son, George." At this point tears fall from Carl's eyes; and Brian, Karen and Jody try give comfort. Carl looks at them with watery eyes and keeps speaking, "My father, George, passed the Golden Seal to me!" Brian, Karen and Jody are spell-bound at Carl's words. Carl stretches out his frail arm holding the object and nods to Jody. She takes the gold piece and firmly clasps her fingers over it. The Grandfather looks tenderly at his granddaughter and comments, "Jody! This is for you!" Jody exchanges eye contact with her dad and mom and exclaims, "For me? - Why? - What about Dad and Mom?" The elderly man glances over at Brian and Karen, then looks at his bewildered granddaughter, and remarks, "Jody! I have a dying request that especially for you! This will help prepare you for Black Eagle." Jody injects, "But Black Eagle is only for the top Ninjans from different tribes!" Carl smiles at Jody and remarks, "You were too young and unskilled before - now, you're ready for the last and most important lesson." Jody asks with eagerness, "What lesson, Grandpa?" Carl responds in a firm gentle tone, "To release your warrior spirit!" Jody leans in close to her Grandfather and speaks lovingly, "Grandpa! You know I'll do anything you ask - What's your special request?" The old man shifts his gaze toward Brain and Karen who are listening intently, then Carl looks sweetly at Jody and comments, "I want you to travel to Japan and return the Golden Seal to the Ninja Clan! It belongs in Japan with its rightful owners - Will you do that for me, Jody? - I planned to return it this Fall (Coughs) Now, my time has run out!" Jody looks directly at her dad and mom, and Brian and Karen smile and nod their support. Jody crouches down eye-level with Carl and firmly clasps his hand, and promises, "Don't worry Grandpa! I'll return the Golden Seal to the Ninja Clan in Japan!" Carl's eyes twinkle with happiness and he gives a contented peaceful smile, and comments, "Each day, I slip away a little more - soon, I'll be gone! There's peace now, knowing the Golden Seal will be returned. (Falling tears) I promised my father to return it, but didn't! (Looks at Jody) Now Jody, you'll return it for me!" The conversation and old emotions have taken a toll on the old man, and Brian leans in with reassuring words, "Rest easy! Karen and I will do our best to help Jody honour your request!" Carl stares at them and softly replies, "I leave all my Ninjan belongings to you to share - The weapons must stay in our family!" Brain nods that he acknowledges and Carl smiles and shuts his eyes - he's very tired. Jody stands beside the bed and looks at her Grandpa laying still. She opens her hand and intently stares at the shiny Golden Seal.

# CHAPTER SIX

*The Funeral*

Bright sunshine covers the country Cemetery the day of Carl's Funeral. The old monuments and gravestones sit nestled amid the manicured grounds. Brian, Karen, Jody and friends gather to say their final farewell. A framed photo of Carl sits atop the lacquered mahogany casket that lays suspended on straps over a freshly dug grave opening. Funeral Home attendants are next to flower arrangements and wreaths set up on both sides of the coffin. A Minister with a thin leather Bible in hand, stands near the top of the grave. People dressed in clothes with black and muted tones are clustered together in a semi-circle facing a black marble headstone that reads…

**CARL LONG GRASS**

Brian, Karen and Jody are in front, each hold a beautiful long stem red rose. Brian also holds a large black eagle feather. Jody quietly sobs and weeps. Karen wraps her arm around Jody to console. Around them, attending friends and supporters each hold a short stem red rose. A Funeral Home attendant nods to the Minister and the Clergyman lifts his thin leather Bible chest-level and begins to speak in a warm and comforting voice, "Dearly Beloved, we are gathered here to say our final good bye to Carl Long Grass - who has been preceded by his wife Kathy Long Grass. (Pause) Carl was a loving husband, a wonderful Father, and an exceptional Grandfather. Carl left this earth while we still remain." A few ladies in the group begin to sob. The Minister pauses slightly, then continues, "He expressed a faith in the Creator and in His Son, Jesus. The Scriptures tell us that God has made a home for Carl in Heaven - where he can dwell with God for all Eternity." The Minister reaches into his jacket and brings out a slender glass tube filled with white sand. He reaches out his arm over the top of the casket and pours the sand into the shape of a Cross and speaks, "Ashes to ashes, dust to dust. We commit our brother Carl's body to the ground. One day, Carl will arise - with no more cancer or pain - But with a Glorified body! That's the Blessed Resurrection!" The Clergyman closes the Bible and steps back. A Funeral Home attendant gently approaches Brian, Karen and Jody and speaks in a hushed tone, "You may say your final Good Bye now." Brian, Karen and Jody step toward the closed casket. A tear runs down Brian's face, Karen's eyes are watery, and Jody quietly weeps. Brian stands frozen for a moment, then he lays the rose and the black eagle feather next to Carl's framed picture. Karen gently places her rose beside Brian's. Jody quietly stares at her Grandpa's portrait - he's healthy, strong and handsome, with a big smile. Jody sniffles as she lays her red rose along side the other two. Brian and Karen put an arm around Jody and walk her back. Once there, they turn and face the grave again. The Funeral Home attendant motions and the rest of the mourners trickle forward to lay their roses on the coffin, then return to their positions. Soon, all the roses lay atop the casket. A Funeral Home attendant tactfully retrieves Carl's portrait. He walks up to the family and hands Brian the framed photo, and speaks softly, "We will be lowering the body at this time. (Pause) Please follow me to the limousine that will be taking you home." The man points the direction with a subtle arm gesture. Brain, Karen and Jody follow the man and leave the graveside. Once the family have departed, the other mourners quietly disperse. Across the Cemetery, the people make their way to parked cars, vans, pickup trucks and SUVs.  The Funeral Home attendant escorts Brian, Karen and Jody to the shiny black Cadillac limousine. The man opens the rear passenger door and Karen, Jody and Brian get in. The attendant respectfully closes the door.

# CHAPTER SEVEN

*A Country Far Away*

The dining table is loaded with cooked food from caring neighbours, friends and community members of the Reservation - fried chicken, tuna casserole, cooked vegetables, mash potatoes, gravy, apple pie, pumpkin pie, a fruit tray, and fresh baked bread. Some family photos sit to one side of the large wood table. Karen, Brian and Jody are eating supper when Jody puts down her fork and picks up a photo of them with Grandpa Carl. She studies at the picture - then looks at her mom and dad and expresses her worry, "I promised Grandpa - but I don't know anything about Japan. And to make matters worse - I've never flown on a plane or even been outside of America before!" The parents exchange glances and Karen replies, "Honey, don't worry about that now - there'll be time to learn about Japan. Your dad and I will help!" Brian adds in, "Your mom's right! We can look at stuff online, find books and even get a Travel DVD about Japan." Her parent's words provide relief and Jody smiles. She picks up another photo of Carl and shows it to them - Carl is in a pink bunny costume. Jody giggles as she remarks, "Remember when Grandpa dressed up as a bunny for my 6$^{th}$ birthday?" Brain and Karen look at the photo and start to chuckle, Brian comments, "Your Grandpa sure went all out for your Birthdays. (Laughs) He ripped that bunny suit because it was too tight." Karen blurts out laughing and remarks, "And I had to sew up that big rip near the tail." Jody takes back the photo to re-examine the picture and asks, "What's so funny about the rip?" By now, Brian and Karen are in stitches laughing. Brian pipes up, "Because mom kept sticking your Grandpa with the sewing needle!" And Karen exclaims, "Afterwards, your Grandpa said - some Birthdays are a pain in the butt!" At this point, all three are sharing a good laugh and pass around more photos as they continue to eat and talk, while having a special family time.

* * *

The day is cloudy and overcast when Jody, Brian and Karen exit their parked car and go inside the Bookstore. They browse the store aisles and merchandise shelves filled with various books. Jody pulls out a large book on Japan. Brian and Karen find othe: books that feature the 'Land of the Rising Sun', and pick out a couple. The trio walk to another area of the store to search the DVD section. Jody finds an interesting DVD on Japan and grabs it. Jody carries the books and DVD, and they head toward the Cashier Counter. Jody sets the items on the counter and the Cashier scans and bags each purchase. The Cashier keys in the Cash Register and asks, "Will that be all?" Jody smiles and answers, "Yes!" The Sales Clerk asks, "And how will you be paying today?" Brian steps up to the counter and presents his bank card and replies, "I'll be paying with Debit!" The Cashier smiles, keys the Sales Terminal and hands it to Briar. He Taps his Debit Card and the electronic terminal hums and cranks out a sales receipt. The Cashier tears off the Merchant's portion, then she hands Brian the Customer receipt, hands over the bag of goods. and comments with a smile, "Thank you! Have a nice day!" Jody takes the purchase bag and the trio walk through the bookstore and exit to the sidewalk near their car by the curb. They get into the vehicle and Brian starts the engine and drives away from the curb and goes with the traffic, heading toward home.

At the house, Jody, Karen and Brian sit on the sofa and watch the DVD on Japan on a large flat screen TV. They see video of modern Tokyo with its sleek office buildings, neon covered streets, crowded subway cars, Buddhist temples, and Bullet trains. The DVD shows them neat uniform school students, traditional Geishas, Japanese cars, high-tech electronics, and Sushi Bars. Jody, Brian and Karen are fascinated at the terraced rice paddies, Oriental architecture, beautiful gardens, picturesque landscape, and magnificent Mount Fuji. Over the next few days and nights, they look through various books, and spend time visiting Japan websites online. As Jody collects information she jots down notes, and spends time flipping through the large travel book on Japan. Brian brings over Carl's extensive research notes, and the trio study the Grandfather's writings and illustrations. Eventually, with enough knowledge and information gathered; Brian and Karen and Jody work on Japan maps and travel plans.

* * *

Brian, Karen and Jody sit at the dining table one evening. Karen and Jody sip their mug of tea while Brian enjoys his cup of coffee. Jody remarks, "Sure wish you guys could join me overseas!" Karen and Brian exchange eye contact and Brian comments, "I'm sorry Jody! I'd love to go but can't - house construction has ramped up and my crew is on a tight deadline." Karen reaches out to clasp Jody's hand and explains, "Sorry honey! I don't have enough seniority with the Nurses' Union. I can't get time off until after January!" Jody cradles her mug of tea and looks at her parents with wistful eyes and sighs, "I know - guess I was just hoping." Brian taps his index finger on the table top to get Jody's attention and to reinforce the point he makes, "You can do it! Your Grandpa knew that better than anyone. - And your mom and I know it too!" Jody looks at her parents and a smile dawns across her face and she remarks, "Grandpa did say it will help me." Her dad nods as he comments, "Your Grandpa understood that somehow going to Japan would teach you - help prepare you for Black Eagle!" Jody's attitude and motivation becomes fortified and she declares, "You're right dad! I'm not going alone - I'm taking all the Ninjan training that Grandpa gave me!"

# CHAPTER EIGHT
*Flying To Japan*

Individuals and groups of people move to and fro through the Airport Terminal. The building interior is busy with Airport workers, Airline Flight crews, Ticket Counter attendants, passengers, family and friends. Travellers holding their luggage join various lineups, many with Boarding Pass in hand.

Jody in jeans and jacket with her stuffed backpack slung over the shoulder, stands beside her upright suitcase that sits on four stubby wheels. She holds a carry-on. Her parents stand nearby. Karen looks at Jody with a melancholy gaze while Brian scans the Departure Display. Her dad remarks, "Jody, it's almost time!" Jody looks at her folks and exclaims, "I miss you guys already!" Karen gives her a big mommy squeeze with comforting words, "As soon as you land - give us a cal! Let us know you're all right!" Jody smiles and nods and hugs mom tight. Brian leans in to wrap his arms around both and gives a group hug. Jody gazes into her parents eyes and assures, "I'll call as soon as the plane lands and I clear Customs." Brian places his hand on Jody's shoulder and speaks in a fatherly tone, "Remember - stick to the plan we made! Follow each step. (Pause) If there's a problem - don't hesitate - call us!" Jody nods her head with a serious look to let her dad know she got the point.

TERMINAL ANNOUNCEMENT CHIMES
   "Boarding Call for United Airlines Flight 252 to Tokyo, Japan,
   at Gate 37 - Passengers can now board the aircraft."

Mom, dad and daughter have one last quick hug. Jody grabs her luggage trolly and steers it toward the Departure Zone. Airport Staff at the entrance check Jody's ticket and wave her through. Karen leans against Brian as they watch Jody go through the Departure Area sliding doors only to disappear behind the frosted glass. Karen looks into Brian's eyes and whispers, "She'll okay, right?" Brian gives his wife a confident look and replies, "Jody can handle herself! I'm more afraid she might end up living in Japan - far away from us!"

Inside the Departure area, Jody stands at the Boarding zone for Gate 37, Flight 252 to Tokyo, Japan. She's in the lineup and moves forward when it's her turn. The Attendant checks Jody's Ticket and motions to go ahead. She joins passengers as they walk the Terminal Gangway to the parked aircraft. As Jody approaches the plane, a Flight Attendant inspects her Boarding Pass and points her down the aisle. Jody shuffles along with the other passengers in the congested cabin aisle as people find their seats and get settled. Jody scans the seat numbers and finds ROW 16 and SEAT A that's next to the window. She reaches up and places her backpack in the overhead storage compartment, shuts the door and gets into her window seat. Jody tucks her carry-on under the seat, buckles up and gets comfortable. As she lifts her eye to watch the other passengers move past her, she sees a middle-aged white couple come down the aisle checking seat numbers. The heavyset man looks at his Boarding Pass and remarks, "Our seats are here!" His wife, a lady with curly red hair that looks exhausted. comments, "Can't wait to sit down - my feet are killing me!" The man puts his hand on his belly, grimaces and remarks, "I think it's best if I take the aisle seat!" His wife nods and squeezes by to take the seat next to Jody. The man hoists their carry-on into the overhead compartment, closes the door and sits down.

CABIN CHIMES. SEAT BELT LIGHT BLINKS.

The couple grab their seat belts and buckle up. The lady turns to Jody with a friendly smile and makes an introduction, "Hello sweetie! I'm Agnes and this is my husband, Harold." Harold leans forward and gives Jody a polite wave and she waves back, and replies, "Hi! My name's Jody." Agnes studies Jody a bit, then she speaks, "Harold and I are taking an Oriental Tour that starts in Japan. (Pause) Are you Japanese?" Jody smiles and replies, "No. I'm not Japanese - I'm an American Indian - from Wyoming!" The lady gets apologetic and explains, "I'm sorry! I thought with your complexion and shiny black hair - you might be a Japanese girl." Jody smiles, shakes her head and responds back, "My Grandfather once told me that sometimes, American Indians can be mistaken for Asians. (Pause) He told me American Indians came across from Asian thousands of years ago." Agnes tilts her head and leans in close and whispers, "To be honest, honey, I wish I had your beautiful hair and tanned complexion!"

## AIRCRAFT CABIN CHIMES

The big airplane engines fire up and the high pitched whirling sound can be heard inside the plane. The cabin interior slightly vibrates as the plane starts to taxi toward the runway. The Stewardesses stand in front of each seat section and begin to go through the Flight Instructions. The aircraft quickly finds its position on the runway and waits for departure clearance from the Airport Controllers. The engines begin to INCREASE THROTTLE. Jody peeks out her window to look across the flat Airport grounds with its many array of coloured lights and painted markings. Suddenly, the engines fire FULL BLAST and the planes begins Take Off. Jody is amazed at how quick the outside ground rushes by as the plane accelerates. Jody notices the cabin interior shakes and vibrates as the plane picks up more and more speed, she sits back in her seat and clutches the armrests with both hands. Agnes looks at Jody's semi-frozen state and remarks, "First time flying?" Jody turns her head and nods, "Yes! I've never been on a plane before." Agnes reaches to put her hand over Jody's hand and comments with a voice of experience, "Take off is the roughest part - soon, it will be smooth sailing." At MAX VELOCITY the entire plane shutters - Suddenly, the plane lifts off and climbs - the vibrations stop. The aircraft ascends at a steep angle and Jody looks out her window at the earth below to see a patchwork of farms, towns, wilderness terrain and sprawling forests. In a few minutes, the aircraft levels off and the SEAT BELT LIGHT goes out. Jody peers down at the snow covered mountains below. Throughout the cabin, many passengers unbuckle and prepare to relax. Jody lifts her head to see people read magazines and novels, parents entertain small children, and others lean back to snooze. Jody leans back in her seat and becomes more relaxed. Suddenly, Harold gets up, grimaces and looks at his wife and remarks, "I need the washroom!" Harold swiftly goes down the aisle toward the washrooms. Agnes turns her head toward Jody and asks, "Are you traveling with your family?" Jody turns toward her fellow passenger, smiles and replies, "No! I'm travelling by myself." The middle-aged woman comments, "Please don't think I'm ncsey, but, why are you travelling to Japan by yourself?" Jody thinks for a few seconds and responds, "I'm going to Japan for research!" The woman's curiosity is peeked and she asks, "What are you studying that you have to fly to Japan?" Jody looks into the woman's eyes and replies, "Something to do with Martial Arts." The woman sits back in her seat and remarks, "Martial Arts!? Isn't that about fighting and hurting people?" Jody makes eye contact and responds, "I've studied Martial Arts since I was young, and I don't believe in hurting people. My Teacher taught me that." Agnes fixes her eyes on Jody, "What if some guys attack or assault you?" Jody leans forward with a determined expression and responds, "They'd wish they hadn't!" Harold ambles back down the aisle and sits down in his seat, looks at Agnes and asks, "Did I miss anything? What were you talking about?" Agnes places her hand on Jody's hand and replies, "Oh, just talking about girl stuff!" Harold shrugs and sits back in his seat. A Stewardess pushes a beverage trolly down the aisle and stops beside them, and politely asks, "Would anyone like a beverage?" Harold looks at the cart and remarks, "Got any beer?" The Stewardess smiles, brings out a bottle and Harold smiles wide.

# CHAPTER NINE

*Narita International Airport*

Narita International Airport is a low modern building made of metal and glass with curved roofs. Two long separate sections jut out at one end, while the other end features two separate circular pods. From the view above, the Terminal layout resembles a stylized Japanese Kanji.

The United Flight 252 descends from its approach position and lands on the long tarmac runway of Narita International Airport, then taxis to the Terminal. The passengers gather their belongings and the Flight Crew oversee and guide them to disembark the aircraft. Jody walks with the other passengers in the enclosed gangway to the Terminal building. Japanese Staff greet them with the customary bow and direct the passengers to the area to clear Customs. The people get into lines and wait as Custom Officials process each traveller. One Customs Agent motions his hand to beckon Jody forward to his location. She reaches the counter and presents her American Passport and Airplane Ticket. The man scans her Passport and Ticket, then presses a Japanese Customs Stamp on a Passport Page and hands it to Jody. She secures the Passport and Flight Ticket in her travel pouch and moves away from the counter toward the revolving Baggage Carousels, to where other passengers await their luggage. After a bit of time watching others get their suitcases and belongings, Jody spots her luggage trolly, picks it off the Carousel and sets it down beside her. The young lady reaches into her jean pocket to bring out a small note card and reads the Travel Points that she and her parents prepared…

1. Clear Customs
    2. Get Japan Rail Pass
    3. Train to Tokyo Station

* * *

Jody pockets the card, adjusts her backpack and grips the carry-on, then she grabs the handle of the luggage trolly and heads toward the Airport Concourse. She scans the JAPANESE/ENGLISH signs placed throughout the Airport for the International travellers. Jody walks into the Terminal passageway and scans the interior and finds the sign pointing toward the Japan Rail Counter. Jody chooses to move through the outer pillars of the Main Lobby to avoid the milling crowds. She reaches the Counter and the lady smiles and bows. Jody takes out her travel pouch, unzips it and takes out 3,000 Yen, hands the money to the Japan Rail Agent and asks, "A ticket to Tokyo Station, please." The lady smiles, collects the bills, bows and hands Jody a One-Way Japan Rail Pass to Tokyo. Jody receives the Pass, nods to the Agent and turns toward the Concourse and follows the signage to the Japan Rail Platform. The glass doors of the Terminal slide open and Jody walks out onto the platform area fitted with scattered benches. She looks around at the others waiting and peers down the tracks and sees nothing but empty rails and arrays of track lights. Jody sits down on a bench and pulls out her phone and an International Calling Card, and dials home and waits - LONG DISTANCE DIAL SEQUENCE - the her mom answers with a sleepy voice, "Hello!" Jody announces with excitement, "Mom! It's me!"

Back on Plains Road, in the raised bungalow, Karen sits up in bed delighted to hear her daughter's voice all the way from Japan, thousands of miles away. She pushed her arm on Brian to rouse him. Brian rubs his eyes and wakes up - Karen puts the phone on Speaker mode, and asks, "Jody - Jody honey - so good to hear your voice! We put you on Speaker Phone. Was your flight okay?" Jody replies, "Bumpy at first but it was fine. I got the Japan Rail Pass, and I'm just waiting for the next train - it's an hour ride to Tokyo Station." Brain leans toward the home phone and remarks, "You all right? - Any problems?" Jody grins and responds, "Everything's fine dad! Following the Plan like we talked about." Her dad nods, smiles and looks at Karen and whispers, "That's our girl!" Karen comments in a motherly tone, "Call us when you get settled in your Hotel room. Let us know that you're safe!" Jody hears the sound of metal train wheels on steel rails and turns her head to see the train approaching. She replies to her mom, "The train is coming - gotta go now. I'll call from the Hotel." Brian calls out, "Remember Jody, stick to our Plan!" Karen adds in, "Stay safe honey. We love you!" Jody responds, "Love you guys! - Gotta run." Jody pockets her phone and grabs the trolly handle as she watches the train pull to a stop beside the platform landing. CHIMES sound as the train doors slide open. As other passengers enter the train to find seats, Jody steps into the passenger compartment and glides her luggage to a row of seats and sits down. She scans about at the Japanese travellers interspersed throughout the train car. CHIMES sound again and the compartment doors WHOOSH shut as the train pulls away and goes down the tracks. Jody watches railway lights and illuminated Japanese ads whiz by. She leans forward enough to glimpse the bright Tokyo City skyline up in the distance. Jody sits back in her seat and takes a deep breath.  The train speeds through dense urban development - buildings, stylish condos, tall slender apartment towers, retail stores, and gleaming corporate office buildings. Jody watches in child-like wonder. She has a momentary flashback to Venture's four-way Stop and the spartan Indian Reservation. Jody looks out as the train approaches busy Tokyo Station with its network of train tracks, lights, switches, passenger trains and coloured platforms. She holds the trolly handle and pulls on her backpack as the train rolls to a smooth stop. CHIMES sound and the train doors open. Jody walks with the fellow passengers along the platform landing and takes the escalator and steers the trolly through the illuminated Concourse of Tokyo Station that is bustling with thousands of commuters, passengers and travellers. She follows the ENGLISH signs and enters the spacious Tokyo Station Lobby with its pillars and circular European style dome several floors high above the mezzanine ground level. Jody stares up at the molded details and decorative features reminiscent of architectural domes she's seen on TV travel shows about Europe. Jody lowers her eye and scans the busy interior and spots the GINZA navigation sign. She steps aside out of the way of the pedestrian flow to pull out the note card.

## 4. YOSAN BAJETTO HOTEL, GINZA

She tucks the note back in her jean pocket and moves in the direction of the passageway marked GINZA. The Concourse is lined with retail stores and Sushi Bars. Many Japanese travellers already carry the small customary gift package to honour the traditional custom of gift giving when visiting family and friends. Jody looks at the pedestrians around her - everyone has jet black hair and oriental complexion. Her eyes dart here and there, only to find one or two Caucasians in the mix. She continues along the marble tiled Concourse until reaching the CENTRAL EXIT doors. The glass doors slide open and Jody steps out to join bustling crowds of people, she has to maneuver and dodge passing people going to and fro on the busy sidewalk. Millions of citizens live in Tokyo City and to Jody it seems like there're all on the sidewalk before her. She glances about and sees to nook in a building exterior that's off the sidewalk and out of the way of the crush of people. Jody moves to the nook, reaching into her backpack and pulls out a folded city map of Tokyo. Her eyes sweep across the streets until she locates the Train Station and the nearby **GINZA DISTRICT**.

# CHAPTER TEN

*Yosan Bejatto Hotel*

Jody traces the route of travel from where she is to the Hotel. She folds
the map up and returns it inside the backpack, then she strikes out to
her destination. Jody walks until she spots the YAESU CHUO-GUCHI
Street sign, turns right and continues along YAESHA-DORI AVENUE
where she notices the various stores. She turns left and goes along
KAJIBASHI-DORI AVENUE to where she sees the **YOSAN BAJETTO
HOTEL** and breathes a sigh of relief.

Jody goes through the entrance doors and steers her luggage inside
and walks up to the Lobby Desk. The female Hotel Receptionist gives
Jody with a warm smile and respectful bow and greets her new guest
in Japanese. Jody smiles and replies, "Sorry! I don't speak Japanese."
The Receptionist smiles and responds in English, "Welcome to the
Yosan Bajetto Hotel!", and gives a polite bow. Jody slides the trolly
close and rests her elbow on the marble counter and remarks, "I'd like
a non-smoking single room for three nights please." The young lady
scans her monitor as her fingers move the mouse across the screen to
highlight a rectangle, then she smiles, "Your room is 10-34. Room #34
on the 10th Floor." Jody takes out her zippered travel pouch and
removes a Credit Card and passes it to the young lady. The
Receptionist inserts the card into a small countertop terminal and
enters keystrokes - ELECTRONIC PRINTING. A paper receipt
emerges. The young lady hands Jody the Credit Card, the Receipt, and
the Hotel Room Access Card. Jody smiles and comments, "Thank you!
(Pause) Arigato!" The female staffer gives a big smile, bows and replies
in English, "You are welcome! Enjoy your stay." Jody puts the Credit
Card and Receipt into the travel pouch and tucks it into her backpack.
She looks about the Lobby - the Receptionist lifts her arm, smiles and

points to the Lobby Elevators. Jody sees the Elevators, turns to nod and smile at the young lady, then steers the Trolly and crosses the marble floor toward the Elevators to press the metal UP Button. CHIMES. The Elevator doors open. Jody enters, turns and pushes the button for the 10th Floor.

Jody pushes her luggage along the carpeted hallway and scans the room numbers. She passes 32 - 33 and comes to Room 34. She takes the Access Card from her jean pocket and inserts it into the door lock mechanism. Green Light. Click! Jody pushes down the lever handle and the room door opens, she moves the trolly through the doorway, shuts the door and locks the deadbolt. Jody turns about and views the clean modern room with its single bed with bedspread and pillow neatly tucked in, and a small desk with a convenient table lamp. Jody steps over to the bed, turns and flops onto the cover. She brushes her hand across the soft mattress and smiles delight. Jody is totally exhausted from travelling thousands of miles - she closes her eyes - and falls asleep.

Some time later…

Jody sits upright on the bed and YAWNS! She stretches her arms and then rubs her eyes, then looks around the room. The luggage trolly is still by the door. Jody gets up, grabs the trolly and lays it flat onto the bed. She spins the combination, pops the latch to swing open the suitcase. Jody opens the dresser drawers and puts away her clothes. Then she shuts the suitcase and stands it next to the wall. Jody zips open her backpack to dig out a Tokyo City Map and spreads it out on the desktop. She eyes TOKYO STATION and the GINZA DISTRICT. Jody takes out her cell phones and notices the time is 7:00 PM. She brings out the International Calling Card and dials. ELECTRONIC TONES.

Across the Pacific Ocean, in Northwest America…

The cell phone BUZZES on the nightstand. Karen grabs it, presses Speaker Mode and shakes Brian to wake up. The mom asks with excitement, "Hello! Jody?" Jody voices comes across clear. "Hi mom! I've checked into the Hotel and got a nice room - but I'm feeling really tired!" Brian stirs alert and leans close to the phone, "That's just the jetlag from your long flight. Rest up, you'll feel better tomorrow." Karen leans in beside Brian to caution her daughter, "Remember our talk! Always keep your travel pouch secure! Big cities have pickpockets, I'm sure it's no different over there." Jody replies, "Mom - don't worry! I'll be on my guard. (Pause) It's so exciting to be here! Tokyo is even better than those Travel Books. Everything is so lively and modern - Nothing like the Reservation!" Brian looks at Karen and remarks, "Why not do the Tourist thing for a couple days - see what Tokyo's like before you go to the Iga Mountains." Jody glances down and runs her fingers across the unfolded TOKYO CITY MAP and responds, "You think that will be okay?" Her mom advises with a motherly tone, "Jody honey - who knows when you'll ever be in Tokyo again? Head out and see the city (Pause) Take one of those Bus Tours." Jody smiles at the idea and replies, "Ok guys! If you think there's time - I'd love to see the sites here!" Jody stands up, walks to the window to part the curtain and look out at the bright city lights. Her eyes sweep across the city skyline filled with illuminated modern buildings. Brian encourages his daughter, "Jody, take a Daily Tour Bus - you can travel inland later on. Go ahead - enjoy yourself! (Pause) Your Grandpa would want you to!" Jody becomes still at her dad's words - then she replies with a wide smile, "You're right dad! Grandpa would be so proud I'm here in Japan doing what he asked! (Pause) Love you guys! Good night!" Her dad responds, "We love you, Jody! Take care. Karen squeezes in a quick good bye, "Love you Jody! Be safe." As the phone call ends, Jody draws close the curtains and steps away from the window. She walks over to set her phone on the small desk, goes to the dresser, opens a drawer and brings out her pyjamas.

# CHAPTER ELEVEN
*Tokyo City*

Bright and early the next day, Jody stands in the Lobby before the female Receptionist to ask, "Where can I get a Tokyo Day Tour Bus?" The young lady picks out a Tourist Brochure, hands it over and comments, "Day Tour Bus! You see Tokyo City on bus. Buy ticket - Tokyo building." Jody holds the Brochure and points to a Map detail to ask, "Is this the address? Can I get the Day Tour Bus there?" The Receptionist scans the Map detail, smiles and nods, "Yes! Day Bus not far. You walk 15 minute - Follow Map!" Jody replies with a smile, "Ok! Thank you! Arigato!" Jody clasps the Brochure, pivots around and walks out the Hotel Entrance to step onto the street outside. She checks the Brochure and heads up **KAJIBASHI-DOR AVENUE**. Jody turns right onto **MARUNOUCHI-DOR** and walks past buildings, stores and retail shops to arrive at the Tokyo Building.

Jody looks around and spots the sign and location for the DAY BUS TOUR. She moves toward the building, enters the Reception Area and approaches the Ticket Counter. She looks up at the overhead sign: DAY TOUR 1,000 YEN. A petite uniformed Ticket Agent at the counter, smiles and gives a bow, "Ohayougozaimasu!" Jody gets her travel pouch and removes 1,000 Yen and remarks, "I'd like a Daily Tour Pass please!" The young female clerk quickly smiles, prints out a **DAY PASS TICKET**, picks out a **BUS ROUTE BROCHURE**, and passes both over as Jody gives the money. The Ticket Agent smiles and politely speaks, "You follow Map - see Tokyo City. Very beautiful!" Jody opens the Map and notices the various Colour Coded Routes, and asks the young lady, "What Route will let me get on and get off to sightsee?" The gal behind the counter opens up a Map from the rack and points to a Route, "**Blue Line**. You stop, get off, get on. - Must use

Blue Line. Very important!" Jody examines her Map, nods and turns to look at the Coloured Bus Stops on the street outside. She looks at the female Ticket Agent, smiles and bows, "Arigato!" The young worker replies in Japanese, "Have a nice day!" Jody pushes open the exit door and steps onto the sidewalk outside. She navigates her way through the busy pedestrians to reach the **BLUE BUS STOP SIGN**, and stands with the DAY PASS in her right hand. She glances around the busy urban environment with gleaming office towers and contemporary buildings, stores and open spaces.

A DAY BUS approaches the Stop and slows to a halt. Jody steps back as all types of passengers exit onto the sidewalk to disperse into the pedestrian crowd. Jody climbs onto the Bus and presents her DAY PASS to the Driver. He looks at the Ticket, smiles and nods. She turns and goes down the Bus aisle and notices stairs that lead to the Upper Deck open-air viewing level. Jody makes her way up the steps to the Upper Deck and strolls the aisle to the middle section to get a seat at the Bus side. She sits down, dons her sunglasses and adjusts the strap to put the travel pouch to her front. Other people get on the Bus - Japanese and International Tourists. Some sit at street level, while others intersperse among the Upper Deck seats. ENGINE REV. The Bus pulls away to merge with traffic. Jody smiles - it's a bright sunny day - perfect weather for sightseeing. As the Bus moves through traffic, the wind blows Jody's long black hair around. After a few moments, the Bus passes **SHIBA PARK** where Jody looks at the red **TOKYO TOWER** for communication. The Driver stops the vehicle at a popular Tourist destination - Jody stands on the grounds near the ancient **IMPERIAL PALACE** with its stone walls. Back in her seat, Jody watches as the Bus goes through **UEDO PARK'S** wide boulevards and stunning flowers beds. The DAY BUS travels along the **SUMIDA RIVER** that flows through Tokyo City, and takes the passengers to the big bustling **TSUJIKI FISH MARKET** - the largest fish market in the world. Jody has never seen so many kinds of fish and is amazed at the variety and the sheer volume. Later, the Bus takes the sightseers to the **SHINJUKU-KU DISTRICT** with its colourful **TRENDY STORES** and noisy **PACHINKO PALORS**. Next, the driver takes the people to see the nearby **WEST SHINJUKU DISTRICT** dotted with prestigious **CORPORATE TOWERS.** Jody looks here and there with wonder. She has a big grin at seeing all the Japanese sites and attractions. Jody checks her Tour Brochure and the Street Map for the **SWORD**

**MUSEUM** near **YOYOGI PARK**. She looks at the upcoming **BLUE LINE STOP - YOYOGI PARK**.

47

# CHAPTER TWELVE

## *The Sword Museum*

Jody stands up and goes downstairs to the rear exit doors of the Day Bus and waits. The Bus pulls up to the Blue Sign and stops. The Exit Doors open and Jody steps out onto the wide sidewalk. After a few seconds, the Bus pulls away and zooms down the road. Jody walks into Yoyogi Park and sees the sign for the **MEIJI JINJU SHRINE** and moves in that direction. She strolls past the Shrine, going further into the Park grounds. Jody is amazed at the colourful flower beds, manicured lawns, picturesque walkways, and the beautiful Japanese Maple, Pine, Oak, and Cherry trees. Yoyogi Park is a stunning natural parkland set within large modern Tokyo. In Jody's mind, she recalls images of the Indian Reservation of Venture set in the desert terrain; surrounded by cactus, sage brush, rock canyons, and rugged wildness. Back home, there's no train stations, malls, office towers, modern boulevards, or crowded city streets. On route through the grounds and cultivated ornamental gardens, Jody stops to admire a grand Cherry Blossom tree with its delicate pink flowers - so lovely - so breathtaking. She takes out the Tourist Map to check the location, turns and resumes her trek to the **Sword Museum**, a definite 'must see' while she's in Japan. Jody goes along the walkway, turns onto **SANGUBASHI**, then continues through a few streets until she spots her destination. Jody approaches the **SWORD MUSEUM**, reaches the front entrance, stops, takes a breath - then she enters inside.

The Sword Museum's First Floor presents the entire Sword Making Process for the education and benefit of the visiting tourists. The visitors can follow illustrated examples of the Stages involved - Raw Materials, Forging Techniques, Shaping, Grinding, Honing, and the finished polished Sword. Jody tours through each stage of the Sword

Making Process. She studies the illustrated displays and reads the descriptions. When she's seen enough, Jody climbs the stairs to the 2nd Floor. The Second Level displays the numerous Swords used through Japan's history. Each Sword is an outstanding masterpiece of traditional Japanese swordsmith artistry and exquisite design. Jody stands amazed as she's surrounded by all the fantastic Japanese Katana Swords. She moves throughout the floor. Every sword she sees, her eyes trace its unique features and design details, the rich colours, the highly polished lacquer, and the exquisite Japanese craftsmanship. Jody is transfixed as she stares at a stunning red Katana sword with an intricate handle and gleaming steel blade. As her eyes get lost on the red sword - for a few seconds, she imagines a Japanese Samurai welding the red sword as he protects defenceless peasants from armed bandits. Suddenly, the sounds of other tourists browsing displays makes Jody snap out back to the moment. She glances around to see the Lower Level staircase and heads downstairs. She exits the Sword Museum and pauses on the steps to gaze at the local neighbourhood. Jody spots some interesting stores up the street and goes to check things out.

Jody walks along browsing shops and casually explores side streets. She turns a corner and walks toward a five story building that features a neon sign - **KOI REN'AI CAPSULE HOTEL**. Five tough looking young men, Japanese HANZAI-SHU street thugs, stand on the sidewalk engaged in conversation and happen to be blocking the way. As Jody approaches and makes eye contact, she gets uncomfortable at the way they leer at her. One young man, the Hanzai-shu Leader, steps in front of her and remarks in Japanese, "What a pretty girl!" Jody stops and is reserved and polite as she replies, "I'm sorry! I don't speak Japanese." The Hanzai-shu leader grins as he looks at the others, then comments in broken English, "You tourist? - American?" Jody cordially responds, "Yes! I'm American." As Jody is focused on the man addressing her, one thug unbeknownst to her uses his cell phone to quickly take her photo. The gang leader eyes Jody and remarks to his companions in Japanese, "Gaijin! - She's very attractive!" The young man next to him comments, "We always need more pretty girls!" The Hanzai-shu leader replies, "Especially Gaijin girls - Worth lots of money!" At this point, Jody feels uncomfortable at the foreign banter and begins to step to the side to go around, "Sorry I don't understand what you are saying - I must go now!" The gang leader smiles, steps back and sweeps his arm with an inviting gesture, A gold bracelet with a tiny snake medallion hangs from his wrist, "Tokyo beautiful city! - You go see." Jody replies, "Thank you! Arigato!" She gives a polite quick smile and briskly walks away down the street, moving past buildings and stores. The five thugs watch her as she goes into the distance. The gang leader looks at his crew and orders, "Follow her. When you get a chance - grab her!" The four street thugs head out in Jody's direction.

Jody walks along admiring the quaint shops - stopping to browse and inspect knick-knacks, crafts, and curious retail items. She turns a corner and goes halfway up a narrow side street - SUDDENLY! - two guys step out from a street on her left, and two guys comes out from a street on her right. Jody is caught in the middle - she braces herself! As the street thugs close in - one guy reaches at Jody and she grabs and torques his arm buckling him to the pavement. The guy behind puts his arms out to snag Jody. She scratches his faces with her nails, spins about with a roundhouse that sends him flying backwards. The four thugs are surprised and one exclaims, "This Gaijin knows Martial Arts!" One gangster pulls out a knife and circles Jody and chimes, "She's just one - We are four!" He steps in to swipe the blade. Jody blocks, sidesteps to unleash a flurry of blows that stops him cold. He collapses! A thug yells out, "All attack now! Get her!" Jody dashes to her left and a thug pursues her. She quickly ducks behind a street lamp and he repeatedly tries to catch her - Jody grabs his arm and forcefully yanks the guy hard against the metal post - CLUNK! He's knocked out and crumples to the ground. The two thugs still standing attack her with knives - one on each side. Jody ducks the knife swipe and pivots to avoid a leg kick. She uses her both arms to grab and wrench the attacker's knife arm. He bellows in agony! Jody turns and kicks the last remaining thug in the crotch - THUD! The hoodlum drops like lead. She scans her foes - two are knocked out, two others wither in pain on the pavement.

LOUD VOICES!

Jody turns to see a group of Hanzai-shu at the far end of the street racing toward her. She dashes down the side-street with all her might - her legs eat up the asphalt. As the group of Hanzai-shu reach their fallen comrades, Jody has rounded the corner to disappear out of sight.

Some of the gangsters help the beaten thugs off the ground. The leader of the reinforcements yells, "You were told to catch the Gaijin!" The fallen thugs, now on their feet, nurse their injuries, one of them remarks, "That Gaijin fought like a demon! She must be a Martial Arts Master!" The Hanzai-shu lieutenant looks down the street where Jody vanished. The other gangsters assemble and stand ready. The lieutenant declares, "The Boss wants her! She can't get far - Remember (He smirks) - She's a Gaijin in Japan!" The leader waves his arm and all the gang give chase. Jody runs through a side street and looks over her shoulder - she sees the gangsters and they start YELLING and run toward her. Jody races past some streets and happens to spot **SANGUBASHI**, she quickly dashes down the road. She sees Yoyogi Park up ahead and runs fast onto the grounds. The Hanzai-shu are on her heels in hot pursuit and follow her into the Park. In the middle of the grounds, Jody stops near a cluster of trees to catch her breath. She lifts her eyes to see the thugs coming toward her. Jody sprints across some loose gravel and takes a tumble - her cell phone slips out of her jeans. Jody jumps to her feet and hightails it out of there, she's unaware the phone has fallen out and lays on the ground behind her. She runs across the parkland to exit Yoyogi Park and keeps on running street after street - until she finds herself in strange surroundings.

# CHAPTER THIRTEEN

## *The Harajuku District*

Jody encounters crowds of Japanese young people that mill about the streets and sidewalks, dressed in colourful trendy clothes with exotic **Harajuku** flare. Everywhere she looks, the young people are dressed like **Fairy Princesses** and **Storybook Characters**, others dress in **Minimalism, Modern Chic,** and **Japanese Anime**, and some wear **black Goth** outfits. Jody turns to look for the gangsters and spots them entering the area. She scurries through the young people, who are either shopping, moving around, or just hanging out in small groups. The Hanzai-shu thugs run into the area and quickly spread out. Jody glances around and notices thick bushes in a concrete planter and ducks behind it, out of sight. Jody is bent down to catch her breath, she lifts her head and makes eye contact with a Japanese young man, **KEI**, sitting on a bench behind her. Kei is dressed as a Harajuku Hipster - black leather jacket, ripped designer jeans, belt with silver metal studs, a wallet chain, checkered shirt, and a French Tam. Kei observes Jody crouched down behind the concrete planter - his eyes convey that he's curious and somewhat puzzled?! Jody looks at him and desperately pleads, "Help me! Please! They're after me." Kei lifts his eyes to see the Hanzai-shu gangsters combing the area checking different groups. He gives Jody a quick glance, looks at the thugs, then extends his arm and motions, "Follow me - I will help hide you!" Jody smiles relief and quickly gets to her feet. Kei and Jody swiftly go to a side street to disappear. Kei takes Jody through some passageways and around corners until they enter a wide open pedestrian area filled with various groups of youth. Meanwhile,...the gangsters keep checking individuals and groups here and there. The thug leader barks, "Find her! She must be here!"

* * *

Over where Jody and Kei are…

Kei takes Jody up to a group of Japanese Goths dressed totally in black. They look at Kei and Jody. Kei scans their faces and explains, "We need your help! Some bad people are after this Gaijin girl. - Will you help hide her?" The Goth youths exchange glances with one another, then a guy steps out, "Bring her into the middle - we will make her look like one of us." Kei senses Jody is alarmed and doesn't understand, so he turns to Jody and remarks, "These kids are going to hide you." Jody gives a tight-lipped smile and nods. The Goths part to make a semi-circle and Kei brings Jody into the middle. The Goths close in around to conceal them. Jody scans their faces and appearance - heavy black lipstick, eye shadow, eye liner and mascara…all black pants, knitted tops, boots, hoodies, jackets, long coats, scarfs and hats. A trio of Goth girls begin to shed some clothes as items for cover. Jody puts on the black baggy pants, black boots, and slips on a long black knit sweater. One gal forms Jody's hair into a bun with a black ribbon, and fastens Black hoop earrings on her. Another puts on black polish on Jody's nails and black bracelets on her wrists. Two other girls apply black lipstick, mascara and eye liner. Jody stands still as they work on her. Finally, one girl put a black floppy hat on Jody's head. The Goth girls step back to admire their handiwork. Jody looks around and all the Goths are smiling at the transformation. Jody looks totally Goth! One of the Goth youth comments, "She's one of us! - GOSU!" Kei positions in front of Jody and remarks with a smile, "No one will know! You look completely different!" Jody looks at her black finger nails, and feels the hoop earrings, and glances at her black boots, pants and wrist bangles. Jody looks around at everyone, smiles and bows, "Arigato! Arigato!" Kei advises her, "You stay with the group - stay quiet, don't speak. I'll be nearby" Kei turns and walks away to mingle with a large group of young people. At this point, some Hanzai-shu thugs enter the pedestrian plaza and begin to check - thugs moving from group to group. The Goths stand in a loose circle. Two Hanzai-shu muscle in among them to check individuals. The thug with visible scratches on his face stands next to Jody. Jody stares straight ahead with a blank expression. The Thug raises his voice. "Have you seen a Gaijin girl?" All the Goths look stone-faced at the two thugs. A Goth youth responds, "As you can see - We are GOSU!" The gangsters give the Goth youth a mean stare. The thug beside Jody looks at her from head to foot (He pauses), then looks away and remarks, "Send word to us if you see the Gaijin girl! There's a reward." The two gangsters leave and hustle back to the other thugs. When they regroup, the Hanzai-shu hasten off and soon go out of sight. Kei walks back to the Goths and Jody utters her relief, "I was so scared they would find me!" Kei remarks, "I'll take you to a friend's house - it's not far - you can stay there." One of the Goth guys smiles and comments, "She can keep the clothes." As Jody and Kei leave the group, Kei turns to the Harajuku Goths, and bows, "Hontoniarigatozaimashita! All the Goths smile and the Goth leader replies, "Ochikara ni narete, Tanoshidesu!" Kei and Jody, who now looks like a Japanese Goth, briskly walk across the plaza toward a street corner and disappear.

The two travel through streets and past shops until they arrive at Kei's friend's place. It's a three story brick apartment building from the 1950's located on a Golden Gai narrow street, surrounded by small bars and noisy Pachinko parlours. Kei's friend's bachelor pad is on the top floor. They enter the building and climb the three flights of stairs. As Kei and Jody stand at the apartment door, Jody scans around at the 50's decor and colour scheme. Kei inserts a key, turns the doorknob and opens the door. He walks in a few paces, turns to Jody and beckons to enter. Jody glances left and right down the hallway, then steps inside. Kei closes the door and locks it and remarks, "This apartment belongs to my friend. He's away visiting his sick mother." Jody steps into the middle of the tiny apartment and sits down on a wooden chair. She turns her gaze to Kei and asks, "Where did you learn to speak English so well?" Kei smiles and replies, "My mother teaches English to Japanese Executives. I grew up with Japanese and English in our home." The young man walks over to the petite kitchenette and grabs a small plastic kettle. Jody comments, "How long will your friend be gone?" Kei replies, "Two weeks! That's how long his holiday time is." He runs the water, fills the kettle and plugs it in. He walks over to look out the window at the street below. Jody leans back in the chair with a sigh - she's perplexed, "Why did those guys chase me? I don't know them! - Never saw them before!" Kei gives Jody a serious look, "Those were Hanzai-shu - what Americans call Gangsters - Street Thugs!" Jody sits up alert and exclaims, "But why were they chasing me?" Kei notes Jody's bewildered expression and replies, "Because You are Gaijin and pretty! They wanted you for human trafficking!" Jody is stunned and shocked - a worried expression comes over her face and she remarks, "How am I going to finish what I'm here in Japan to do?" Kei steps near and sits in the opposite chair - with curiosity he asks, "Why are you in Japan?" Jody looks into his inquisitive eyes. She reaches into her travel pouch to bring out a small bundle and slowly unfolds the cloth to reveal the Golden Seal. Kei's eyes widen like saucers as he stares at the gold object with its engraved details and indentations. Jody comments, "I promised to honour my grandfather's dying request - to return the Golden Seal to its Ninja Clan!" She reaches out and places the Golden Seal into Kei's open hand. He closely examines the engravings and details, and runs his fingers over a Japanese Kanji. Kei looks at Jody and points, "This means Shinobi - the Japanese word for Ninja! These other words mean - Wealthy Puzzle! - it's like a riddle!" Jody becomes excited and responds, "My grandfather said the Golden Seal is a Key to a **secret Ninja Treasure**!" Kei's eye brows raise and his eyes widen, "Japanese folk stories tell of the Ninja hiding their gold and riches deep in a mountain cave, but no one knows its location! Over the years, many have tried and failed." Jody holds up the gold object and remarks, "My grandfather said this will help find the secret treasure and open the way!" Kei sits back, rubs his chin and ponders a few seconds, then declares, "I will help you keep your promise to your grandfather. What you seek to do is very important and special - Japanese call it - **BUSHIDO**! The way of the **SAMURI** - the **Way of HONOUR**!" Jody smiles and leans forward, "Thank you for your willingness to help me! My parents and I made plans - I must go to the **Iga Mountains**." Kei smiles widely and nods his head, "Many Japanese know the old legends - the Iga Mountains were the ancient home of the Ninja! - I will take you there." The kettle WHISTLES. Kei goes to the Kitchenette and collects two cups. He opens a canister and puts a scoop of tea leaves in each cup - then pours the hot water. As Jody stands up to stretch, Kei walks over and hands her a cup of tea. Jody cradles the cup, slowly sips and sits back down. She comments, "This tastes so good! Thank you!" Kei sits down in his chair and remarks, "Most tourists are in hotels. What hotel are you staying at?" Jody takes another sip and replies, "The Yosan Bajetto Hotel in the Ginza District." Kei stands to his feet and goes over to open a closet to rummage around inside - he steps back holding a medium size backpack in hand, "I packed some clothes for the trip - we can go to your hotel and get your things."

Jody stands up to check for her phone. She pats her jean pockets -

nothing - she gets alarmed! Kei sees her concern and asks, "What's wrong?" Jody checks her pockets again, then quickly sifts through her backpack, "My phone! It's missing! (Pause) I must have lost it when I fell running!" Kei brings over his phone - opens the screen, touches it a few times, then passes it to Jody, "I switched it to English so you can use it." Jody smiles her gratitude, "Thanks! I really appreciate it!" Jody takes the phone, retrieves the International Calling Card from the backpack - and dials home. A BUZZ from the overseas call lights up Karen's phone on the bedroom night stand, she picks it up. Jody's voice carries through, "Hello! Mom, Dad. - It's me!" Karen shakes Brian awake and he rubs his eyes. Karen presses Speaker Phone and responds, "Jody, honey! We were wondering when you'd call. How was the Bus Tour?" Jody replies, "It was nice - saw some really cool stuff. (Pause) Mom, dad, I lost my cell phone!" Her dad leans close and remarks, "That's okay Jody, don't worry about it! We can cancel your phone from this end - no problem!" Jody is glad at her dad's words, "That's a relief! (Pause) Mom. Dad. I met a friend - Kei. He speaks English and Japanese, and is helping me with Grandpa's request." Karen smiles and Brian comments, "Jody - be careful! Stick to our plan and stay safe, okay!" Jody responds, "I'm following the Plan, dad! (Pause) Being cautious and taking care of myself!" Her dad remarks, "Good Jody! Keep in touch - let us know what's happening. Remember - we believe in you! You can do it!" Jody feels encouraged and replies, "I know dad - Thanks! (Pause) I really love and miss you guys!" Karen leans in over the phone, "And we love and miss you too!" Jody closes off, "Bye for now - We'll talk later." Her parents call out in unison, "Bye honey! We'll wait for your call!" With her call ended, Jody hands the cell phone back to Kei and comments, "Thanks Kei! I appreciate that so very much!" Kei pockets the phone and moves to the apartment window to peek at the street below. Jody asks, "Is it safe to go? What about those gangsters?" Kei peeks out the window again and replies, "We can use the backstreets to the Hotel - get your things - then leave your stuff here!" Kei slings on his backpack and Jody puts on her knapsack, and they both exit the apartment. Kei and Jody descend the three flights of stairs, leave the building and take a nearby alleyway. Kei and Jody sneak through the backstreets to reach the Yosan Bajetto Hotel. Soon, they stand outside the door of room #1034. Jody inserts the Access Card to open the door and they both go in, close and lock the door. After quickly gathering her things, Jody with backpack and carry-on, and Kei with the luggage trolly, enter the Hotel elevator. Back on the side streets and back alleys, Kei and Jody peek around corners to see if the coast is clear. Tracing their way back through the backstreets and passageways, soon, Kei and Jody bring the items into the friend's small apartment. Jody gets certain things and re-supplies her backpack. Kei takes Jody's belongings and stores them out of sight in the closet.

# CHAPTER FOURTEEN

*Journey To The Iga Mountains*

At the Hanzai-shu Headquarters, the assembled thugs stand around with nervous expressions. Each hoodlum wears the gang's bracelet that has a small medallion featuring a snake. The Boss, the Hanzai-shu Leader, paces back and forth in anger. He abruptly pivots and points his finger at his henchmen and bellows, "You let a little girl - a Gaijin girl escape! You're not gangsters - You're school children!" One man timidly steps forward and bows low to remark, "The Gaijin girl defeated all our attacks - we were outmatched! She's a Martial Arts expert!" The Leader glances at his gang and all the thugs nod their heads in agreement. The Gang Leader forcefully stomps his foot and holds up his cell phone. He pans his arm to display - JODY'S PHOTO - and sternly orders, "Put the word out! Hunt down the Gaijin girl! Whoever finds her will get a large reward!" The group of thugs nod at each other with sneers and ghoulish grins. The Hanzai-shu Leader strides across the room to a set of Samurai swords mounted on the wall. He grabs the Katana, pulls out the blade and raises the long sword in his hand. The man turns and tilts the polished steel blade back and forth - admiring the shiny razor sharp lethal edge. A gang lieutenant steps out from the ranks and snaps a bow, "You will get the Gaijin! No one escapes you." The Boss looks at the thug, then fixates on the steel blade, and remarks, "This Gaijin needs someone special! - Someone who has never failed us! (Pause) Time for our KOROSHI-YA……our Professional Killer!" The gang members exchange glances and gloat with smug sneers.

Jody and Kei are at the Train Counter to purchase two Tickets to ride the SHINKANSEN - the famous Bullet Trains of Japan. As Kei passes over the money for the fare, the Attendant hands two Tickets to Koyoto

- then politely bows. Kei gives Jody her Ticket who securely stores it in her zippered travel pouch. They walk to the Departure Platform and wait with the other passengers. CHIMES. The sleek glossy Bullet Train approaches and quietly stops. Jody and Kei, each with backpack, enter the Compartment Car and get seated in the front right section. Soon, passengers fill all the available seats of the Train Car. CHIMES. The Shinkansen rapidly pulls away from the Platform and quickly zooms along the track. Jody looks out the window to watch Tokyo buildings, parks and suburbs zip by. She glances at Kei to ask, "How fast are we going?" Kei peers out the window as the cityscape flies by, and replies, "200 Kilometers per hour!" Jody has an alarmed expression and remarks, "Won't we fly off the tracks?" Kei grins, sits back to relax and reply, "Bullet trains do not run on rails like other trains. Shinkansen move by magnetic levitation! The train doesn't touch the ground. Very safe! Very fast!" Jody's eyes widen - she sits back in her seat and looks around the compartment. Fellow Japanese passengers sit back to relax, read magazines, watch video on cell phones, eat snacks - or just snooze. Jody seems to have just settled in when Kei announces their destination approaches. In a matter of minutes, the Bullet Train comes to a smooth stop at the Train Station Platform. Jody scans her eyes across the structure's interior and sees the sign: KOYOTO STATION. The train doors open and passengers flood out to stream along the Platform. Kei and Jody walk with the moving throng. Up ahead, a Kyoto young thug stands next to a building post on the Platform. The thug lifts his head and is stunned to see Jody walk by. He quickly brings out his cell phone to check Jody's Photo - then swiftly dials the Hanzai-shu Leader to inform, "She's here! The Gaijin girl is in Kyoto! Some hipster guy is with her." The Gang Leader orders, "Follow them! Tell me where they go. - We'll send someone!" The young man with cell phone to ear, gives a slight bow and replies, "Hai!"

Jody and Kei arrive at the Kyoto Bus Terminal amid the groups and individuals seeking travel to various points. The Buses are parked in marked-off coloured destination zones. Kei and Jody purchase Bus Fare and watch the passengers disembark as new passengers stand ready to board the vehicle. The Bus Drivers sit in command behind the steering wheels. Jody and Kei climb onto the Bus, show their Tickets, and find seats in the vehicle's middle - Jody gets the window seat and Kei gets the aisle. Off to the side away from the passenger loading zones, the young thug watches them as he lurks behind an

Advertisement board. The Kyoto gangster looks at the display above the Bus's large front window - the LED lights read - IGA MOUNTAINS. The Bus Terminal is busy and noisy. The young thug brings out his cell phone to dial and brings it close to his ear. At the Hanzai-shu Headquarters, the gangsters relax and chill out - some play cards, a few flip through magazines, and others stand to smoke cigarettes and talk. The Hanzai-shu Leader sits comfortably in a overstuffed leather Club Chair. His cell phone lays on a nearby table. It BUZZES - he answers and hears the Kyoto thug's voice, "The Gaijin and her hipster friend are on a Kyoto Bus to the Iga Mountains!" The Gang Leader sneers and remarks, "Good! Wait there until our Associate arrives on the Shinkansen. Show him the Bus Route they took!" The Kyoto thug replies, "Hai! I will be here." The Gang Leader ends the call and stands to his feet. All the gangsters rivet their attention to their leader. He points to a nearby lieutenant and gives an order, "Call the KOROSHI-YA! (Professional Killer) Tell him to go to the Kyoto Bus Terminal. He is to bring the Gaijin to us - if she refuses - then kill her!" The lieutenant snaps a bow, "Hai!"

Somewhere in Chino City……a modern upscale white stucco and black timber bungalow sits surrounded by traditional Japanese landscaping - sculpted shrubs, trimmed trees, pruned flower bushes with arrayed rocks and stones in raked gravel beds. The home is a western style bungalow blended with traditional Japanese gardens - this is the home of the professional killer! The Koroshi-ya is a fit middle-aged man of above average height with grey streaks in his black slicked-back hair, his face is hard and chiselled - befitting his deadly trade. He stands in the living room and walks to a back room where Katana swords of various colours hang on the wall. The man opens the back room's sliding door and steps out onto the polished wood deck that overlooks a picturesque oriental garden. His eyes glance at the beautiful flowers, manicured grass, red Japanese Maples, and water pond filled with Koi fish.

CELL PHONE BUZZ

The Koroshi-ya pulls out his phone to listen to the Hanzai-shu lieutenant at the other end, "There is a Gaijin girl you must bring to us! Go to the Kyoto Bus Terminal - our man will meet you at the Train Station." The killer's cell phone vibrates and he looks the screen -

JODY's PHOTO. The Contract Killer studies Jody's picture and facial features, then responds, "A Gaijin? I've always hunted rival gangsters - but never a Gaijin girl!" The Hanzai-shu lieutenant remarks, "This girl needs your special skills - She's a Martial Artist! If she will not cooperate - Kill her!" The Man's eye brows raise and his eyes widen, he demands, "Tell your Boss - I want triple my regular fee! You will have her soon!" The Koroshi-ya ends the call and goes into the back room, strides over to a glossy white Katana sword to snatch it off the wall. The Killer pulls out the sword blade to masterfully twirl and repeatedly slice the air. His eyes zero in on the highly polished steel and the razor sharp blade. The Assassin turns his gaze to the wall with three rows of white knotted Japanese funeral cloths, each knotted cloth hangs on a wooden peg. The Koroshi-ya has a flashback to when he killed someone - he would hang a white knotted funeral cloth as a Kill Trophy. The man stares at the last peg - it sits empty.

# CHAPTER FIFTEEN

*Searching The Ancient Past*

The Bus leaves Kyoto City behind and enters the countryside. Jody and Kei look out the bus window at the passing terrain. - small villages, rural dwellings, farms, crops, fields and trees. The vehicle travels winding roads as it ascends to higher elevation. Jody gets her backpack, reaches inside to bring out some folded papers. She turns to Kei and comments, "My Grandpa Carl studied Japan for many years. I have his research notes about Ninjas in the Iga Mountains. You can look at them." Jody hands the notes to her friend, and Kei sees the papers are a rich mix of research details, hand drawn illustrations, Japanese Kanji and personal notes. He slowly peruses the findings and notices a sketch of a cave sealed with a massive metal door and lock with the Japanese Kanji TAKARA (Treasure) written beside it. Kei comments, "I've never seen this information before. It's wonderful!" Jody leans to peer closer, "My parents and I tried to figure things out - but couldn't! What do these Japanese characters mean?" She points to a trio of Japanese Kanji. Kei's expression is intense as his eyes closely examine the script - then his eyes brighten as he breaks into a big smile, and remarks, "The first word is NAZO which means puzzle or riddle. The second character is GESENAI - meaning inscrutable or incomprehensible. (Pause) The last word is MAMOTTA which translates - protected." Jody is awe-struck and takes a few seconds for Kei's explanation to sink in, then she talks excitedly, "Puzzle. Incomprehensible. Protected. The Ninja treasure is in a secret cave that no one can find. That makes it incomprehensible. It's protected by a great metal door and lock - and my Grandpa always said - the key to the puzzle is the Golden Seal!" Kei leans back with a big smile in amazement. Then he looks at Jody with a serious expression, "You cannot tell anyone else about the Golden Seal! Your life would be in great danger - many would try to kill you to get hold of it!" Jody stares at Kei with a frozen look and remarks, "Would you try to take the Golden Seal?" Kei takes offence at the question, sits forward and sternly replies, "If I wanted to - I could have easily turned you over to the Hanzai-shu." He locks eyes with Jody and continues, "The gangsters saw me with you. My life is in danger too! (Pause) After you return the Seal and go back to America - I'm still here in Japan - still in danger from the gangsters." Jody's defensive expression changes to meekness and she sincerely apologizes to her friend, "Kei. I'm sorry for thinking that way about you! You've been more than good and helpful to me from the start. (Pause) Please accept my apology? - GOMEN'NASHI!" Jody bows low and hold that position. Kei looks tenderly at his companion and extends his arm to gently raise Jody's face and he smiles, "I accept your apology! Please know we are together in this quest you promised your grandfather. We are what Japanese call - NAKAMA - partners. Buddies!" Jody is greatly relieved at Kei's words and gives him a big hug. They both sit back in their seats with a renewed sense of friendship and shared purpose.

At the Kyoto City Train Station, the Shinkansen whooshes to a stop, the passenger doors open and out steps the Koroshi-ya dressed in a medium grey suit, carrying a long slender case. He stands on the platform and scans about - he's an imposing figure. The young thug hastens up to the man, stops within a few feet and bows waist-level. The older man eyes the younger and orders, "Show me to the Bus Terminal and the Route the Gaijin took!" The young man promptly replies, "Hai! It is not far - you will be there soon." The Koroshi-ya strides forward with confidence. The young thug follows subservient behind the man. In short time, they enter the interior of the Bus Terminal and the Kyoto thug bows and points his hand toward the boarding zone for MEI PREFECTURE - IGA MOUNTAINS. The Assassin looks at the parked bus ready for upcoming departure. He extends Japanese currency in his hand - the young thug bows and receives the money with both hands outstretched. The Koroshi-ya barks, "Buy me a round trip Ticket!" The young gangster bows again and quickly replies, "Hai!", then races off toward the inside Ticket Counter.

As the Bus climbs higher and higher in evaluation, Jody and Kei see a quaint village sprinkled amid the hilly mountain terrain. The traditional Japanese wood houses resemble a bygone era. Village residents quietly go about their daily chores and activities. The Bus stops on a flat stretch of the tarmac, and Kei and Jody disembark to stand on the dirt roadside. The Driver shuts the door and the Bus zooms off and the duo look around at the scattered wooden dwellings. Jody scans to her right and notices an elderly lady sitting on her porch in the shade. Jody taps Kei's shoulder and comments, "Let's try her?" Kei and Jody walk up to the house and respectfully bow before her. Kei politely asks, "Grandmother, do members of the old Shinobi Ninja Clan still live here?" A smile comes across the old lady's wrinkled friendly face and she replies, "I do not know any Shinobi. But you are welcome to ask the other villagers." Jody and Kei glance around at the small homes that dot the rolling hillside. Kei turns to the elderly woman and bows, "Arigatou gozaimasu!" The old lady smiles and nods. The two friends turn and begin to walk up a winding gravel path to a set of homes on a terraced level. Jody looks around the mountain setting, marvels and remarks, "Imagine! This is the very ground where the ancient Ninja lived! Wow!" Kei stops walking to observe the vista and nods, then he waves his arm for them to move on. They reach the first house. Jody looks expectantly at Kei, and he gives an encouraging grin - steps to the front door and lifts his hand - KNOCK! KNOCK! Inside the wooden home there's the shuffling of feet, then an elderly man opens the door and squints at the two young people standing before him. Kei steps forward, bows and respectfully asks, "Grandfather, are there any Shinobi living here?" The old man grins with a twinkle in his eye and replies, "Shinobi is a very old name! No one here has that name." Kei glances over to Jody with a disappointed look. Kei asks further, "Grandfather, can you think of anyone that might answer our question?" The old man rubs his fingers on his chin, shakes his head and responds, "I know of no one. (Pause) But you can still ask the others." Kei bows to the elderly man with expressed gratitude, "Arigatou gozaimasu!" The old man nods, smiles and closes the door. Jody moves beside Kei to enquire, "What did you find out? Any Clan members here?" Kei looks at his friend and replies with a sad expression, "These old people can't help us - they don't know anything?" Jody ponders a second, then remains undeterred, "Let's keep asking - we're right here in their ancient home!" Kei sighs - he points to a row of dwellings on the opposite hillside, and comments, "We can try there!" The two walk down the grade, across the road pavement, and up the winding gravel path that leads to the other buildings. The pebble trail leads them between large boulders on each side. Kei and Jody tread the stone pathway through the big rocks to the terrace area above. They walk to the first house of the tiny row. Kei steps onto the small veranda and KNOCKS! A few seconds later, a middle-aged man stands in the door's threshold and eyes them both. Kei bows and asks, "Uncle, do you know anyone here related to the Shinobi Clan?" The man thinks for a moment, steps forward to point toward the end of the homes and comments, "The last house! A lady from the city moved here three years ago - the house belonged to an old woman - the family name was Shinobi!" Kei bows to reply, "Arigatou gozaimasu!" Kei lifts upright, smiles at Jody, grabs her elbow and urges her to go along the row of homes. Jody is surprised and curious, "What did he say?" Kei replies with delight, "A Shinobi survivor lives in the last house!" Jody exclaims with excitement, "At last! A Ninja Clan member!" The man in the first house watches as they hasten toward the last house, he shakes his head, steps back inside and shuts the door. As Jody and Kei get closer, Kei remarks, "A woman is in the last house, someone with the name Shinobi." Jody looks at her friend and comments, "Let me knock. It might be better if the woman sees it's a young lady!" Kei nods agreement and steps to the side. Jody steps onto the small porch, stands in front of the door, lifts har hand - and KNOCKS! The muffled clatter of Japanese wooden slippers gets louder - then stops. A middle-aged woman dressed in a Kimono with pinned up hair, opens the door and looks at Jody with a surprised expression. She glances over at Kei and he bows and remarks, "This Gaijin girl is looking for any survivors of an old Ninja Clan. - Is your family name Shinobi?" The lady politely smiles then shakes her head, "My family name is Suzuki! I came here to help my grandmother but she died last year." Kei turns to Jody with a dejected look, then bows to the woman in the doorway, "Aunt. Arigatou gozaimasu!" Jody and Kei turn and start to walk away when the woman interjects, "My family name is Suzuki, but my elderly uncle is a Shinobi!" A big grin breaks out on Kei's face and he looks at Jody, "She has an uncle that's a Shinobi!" Jody quickly spins about to gaze at the lady in the kimono and remarks, "Ask about her uncle's house?" Kei moves his eyes to the lady and asks, "What house is your uncle's?" The woman's face becomes sad as she replies, "My uncle no longer stays here in the mountains. He lives in the SAGA REGION near the sea. He makes pottery!" Kei asks further, "What pottery town does your uncle work in?" The lady ponders a couple seconds, then responds, I cannot tell you because I do not know. (Pause) But I can give you a sample of his ceramic artwork. Each potter has their own style - you can look for his work." The woman suddenly disappears from view - Jody and Kei can hear the sounds of rummaging. The lady quickly returns to the doorway holding a small ceramic bowl that features surging blue waves and swirling white clouds. She passes the bowl to Kei. Jody and Kei examine the fine quality and beautiful pattern. Kei lifts his eyes to the woman and bows - Jody follows suit. Kei speaks their gratitude in Japanese, "Aunt. Thank you very much for your help!" The lady smiles, turns to go inside, and closes the door. Kei steps beside Jody with a big smile, Jody asks, "What did she say? What is it?" Kei replies with delight, "She said her uncle carries the name Shinobi. He lives in the Saga Region near the coast (shows bowl) and makes this kind of pottery." Jody inspects the bowl again with excitement, "Fantastic! All we have to do is go look for him." Kei looks into her eyes, "It might be difficult. The area has four towns famous for pottery. We might have to visit each town!" Jody clutches Kei arm in her exuberance, "We're so close! Let's go and finish what we started!" Kei nods and safely stores the small bowl in his backpack. They begin to walk back down the pebble walkway that leads between the big boulders on either side.

# CHAPTER SIXTEEN

*Menace in the Mountains*

As the Jody and Kei retrace their steps and go between the large boulders - Suddenly, the Koroshi-ya steps out from seclusion and holds a drawn Katana sword. The man waves the shiny steel blade across their path, beckons with his free hand as he utters broken-English, "Gaijin! Young girl - go Tokyo! Now!" Kei automatically freezes with his mouth open. Jody stares at her foe and slips off her backpack - it falls on the stones with a THUD! Jody quickly warns her friend, "Kei. Quick! Turn around and run!" Kei looks at Jody, nods and bolts out of there as fast as his leg can carry him. Now, just the two of them are on the stone pathway in the middle of the boulders. Jody and the Koroshi-ya lock eyes - both stand ready!

The professional killer lowers the sword blade and holds it at his side pointed to the ground. The man extends his open hand as an invitation. Jody shakes her head and begins to back up to create space between her foe. She watches poised and alert, her arms positioned for battle. Jody stays focused on the man as she backs up against the rock wall. The Assassin's eye brows furrow and his face contorts in anger. He bellows loud in Japanese, "Insolent Gaijin girl! I will take you to Tokyo - alive or dead!" The Koroshi-ya lunges and swings the Katana blade at her. Jody leaps up and uses her leg to spring off the rock to summersault and land behind the surprised man. He swiftly pivots around and Jody kicks hard at the loose gravel on the ground. Pebbles and dirt forcefully spray the man's face. He instinctively raises his arm and closes his eyes. In the distraction, Jody bolts toward some tall slender trees at the end of the boulders. The man wipes debris from his face and gives chase. Jody grabs a sapling and uses her arms and knee to snap the young tree into a crude wooden staff. As the man rushes up, Jody spins and twirls the staff about her torso and locks into a Martial Arts defensive stance. The Koroshi-ya edges closer with caution. He sways the sword blade from side to side. Jody's eyes follow the sword's movement. She quickly scans around and yells, "My friend, I hope you listened and took off!" There's an echo in Kei's voice as he replies, "Still here! I cannot leave you alone." The killer lifts his head to look around at where the voice came from. He refocuses his energy at Jody and prowls back and forth in a semi-circle. The Assassin tilts his head upward and roars, "Tokyo hipster! After I kill your Gaijin friend - I'm going to slice you up in tiny pieces!" The man shifts his eyes onto Jody. He swiftly lifts the sword with both hands and slashes. Jody swings the staff against the sword blade. The man repeatedly slashes - Jody uses the pole to block and deflect the attacks. In seething anger, the Assassin swipes the sword at the young girl's face and head. Jody ducks and swings the pole to knock the blade sideways. She spins the staff and strikes the arm that holds the blade - the sword drops! The Koroshi-ya grabs his elbow which is in great pain. Jody swiftly plunges the staff into his stomach, then snaps the pole upward to hit his chin sending his head backwards. The man falls to the ground with a bloody mouth. Momentarily stunned, he lays on the ground - his grey suit dirty, ripped and torn. The man shakes his head alert and shifts to rise on one knee. Jody holds the staff in an overhead strike position. She looks at him and shifts her eyes to the ground, her foot is on top the Katana sword on the ground. The man raises his arm and waves his hand side to side to feign surrender! Jody watches him like a hawk. As the man slowly gets to his feet, he reaches behind his back to bring out a big knife. He lunges at Jody and the blade just grazes her right outer thigh. Jody powerfully slams the staff across the man's head that drives his skull hard into the rock surface. The tremendous blow stuns and drops him. He GROANS! Jody picks up the white Katana and points the blade at Koroshi-ya and shakes her head - No! She watches as the man props himself up against the rock. Jody remarks in an angry voice, "Stop! No more! - Leave me alone!" Jody holds the sword in one hand as she leans the staff against the rock surface, with her free hand she picks up her backpack, then she grabs the staff again. She carefully backs up as she keeps her eyes on the downed assailant. The man is wounded, worn down and winded. He watches as Jody holds the weapons and backs further and further away until she clears the stone pathway between the boulders.

Jody scans about the hillside and surroundings as she moves down toward the roadway. At the pavement, she moves her gaze around and spots Kei who is peeking around the corner of a house. Kei's eyes light up and he races out from his hiding place. He rushes up to Jody, looks at the katana and exclaims with excitement, "You beat him! You won!" Jody keeps the sword at a downward angle, and partially leans on the staff, and replies, "I remembered my Grandfather's teaching! How your weapons can be in nature - like gravel and trees." Kei glances at the killer's white Katana and grimaces, "I'm Japanese, but I don't like swords - so sharp and dangerous! (Grins) I prefer video games - much safer." Jody lifts the white Katana in the air - the blade gleams in the sunlight. She remarks, "My Grandfather said - swords are neither good or bad - it depends on the person holding the blade!" In the distance, there's the sound of a BUS ENGINE. Kei looks down the tarmac and comments, "Another bus approaches. We can wave down the driver and show our Return Tickets." Jody gives the staff a quick look and tosses it aside - then she eyes the exposed Katana blade, and remarks, "Will the driver let us on the bus with this?" Kei smiles and takes off his jacket to wrap and cover the blade. He replies, "It will be okay with the driver. This is Japan - everyone respects and values our history - especially Japanese swords!" They watch as the Kyoto Bus looms larger on approach. Kei steps onto the pavement and waves the driver to stop. The bus slows to a stop, the side door opens and the driver peers down at them. Kei and Jody ascend the steps and present their Return Tickets. Kei shows the wrapped Katana and the driver nods. Kei and Jody moves through the aisle to grab two seats near the back. The driver shuts the side door, presses the gas pedal and the vehicle motors forward. The bus continues its journey over the serpentine roadway of the Iga Mountains. Kei and Jody watch the rolling mountainside, vegetation and wooden homes.

Up the hill, off to the side, stands the Koroshi-ya in his torn dirty grey suit. He watches the bus motor further and further down the road. He brings his hand up to his face, and he glides his fingers over the large red welt on his forehead. The man turns about and makes determined strides up the pebble pathway toward the row of tiny wooden homes. Soon, the Assassin stands outside a wooden house and lifts his bruised scraped hand - KNOCK! KNOCK! KNOCK! There's the sound of approaching footsteps and the door latch CLICKS. The woman in the Kimono holds the door open with one arm as she stands in the doorway. She scrutinizes the stranger standing before her. The

Koroshi-ya steps forward with an intense stare, and declares, "Two young people visited you - what did you tell them?" The lady looks at the man's dirty ripped clothes, and the red welt on his forehead. She becomes anxious and replies, "They were just tourists - I told them nothing." The man rebuffs her with a stern voice, "I don't believe you! I know you said something - what was it?" The woman gets nervous and starts to shut the door. The Koroshi-ya swiftly barges in to push the door wide open - he looms in the doorway. The woman backs up into the home interior and remarks in a trembling voice, "I live in this tiny village - I know nothing!" The man steps through the doorway into the room and scowls. He yells at the terrified woman, "You say you know nothing - but I have ways to make you talk!" The Assassin gives the lady a menacing look, the lady SHRIEKS as he pulls out his large knife and slowly shuts the door.

Miles away, on the Bus ride back to Kyoto City, Jody turns her gaze to Kei and politely asks, "I'd like to use your phone again to call home. Is that okay?" Kei smiles and brings out his cell phone and hands it over. Jody smiles and pulls out the International Calling Card and dials home. Across the Pacific Ocean, Karen's cell phone BUZZES on the night stand next to the bed - still asleep she fumbles around to grab the phone. Karen blinks her sleepy eyes open and answers. Jody's voice fills her ear, "Mom. Dad. - It's me!" Karen's eyes open wide at hearing her daughter's voice and she stretches out her arm to shake and rouse Brian - he stirs awake. Karen replies, "Jody honey! How lovely to hear your voice. How are you sweetie?" Jody glances over at Kei and responds, "I'm okay! Wanted to call to tell you guys I got great news!" By now, Karen has put Jody on Speaker Phone so Brian and her can listen and speak. Brian echoes Karen's interest and asks, "What's the news Jody?" As the bus winds its way down the curves and straight stretches of the highway, Jody looks at Kei and replies, "Someone in the Iga Mountains gave us valuable information. Right now, we're following a lead to find a Shinobi survivor!" Brian and Karen share big smiles and Karen remarks to her daughter, "Jody, that's wonderful! We're so proud of you! (Pause) And your Grandpa would be so proud of you also!" A tear forms in Jody's eye as she hears her mom's reply. With emotion in her voice, Jody tenderly conveys, "I miss you guys very much! (Pause) And I miss Grandpa too!" Kei notices Jody's teary eyes and puts his arm on her shoulder as comfort. Jody looks at Kei and comments to her parents, "We're going to travel to the Saga area in

Southern Japan. The Ninja Clan survivor is in that region." In their bedroom, on Plains Road in the Indian Reservation of Venture, Brian and Karen send their love and support to Jody over the phone, her mom admonishes, "Please be careful Jody! Be wise and stay safe!" and Brian enquires, "Any problems? You're okay right?" Jody lowers her eyes to the white Katana wrapped in Kei leather jacket, and tactfully replies, "I'm okay, dad! Everything is under control." Her parents' faces show relief at Jody's words and breath easy. Jody eyes Kei and remarks, "Better go now. - I'll call again later. Love you guys! Bye." Karen and Brian lean over the cell phone and reply as loving parents, "We're looking forward to your next call. We love you too, Jody! Bye." Jody touches the phone screen to end the call, and hands the phone back to Kei. She gives a big smile and comments, "Arigato! I really appreciated using your phone so I could call home!" Kei leans back in his seat and replies, "It's good to call your parents - especially when you're thousands of miles away. (Pause) The Japanese believe it's very important to honour your parents!" Jody smiles and comments, "My Grandpa told me the Bible teaches the same thing!"

# CHAPTER SEVENTEEN

*Trouble Back Home*

Brian and Karen are in the pickup truck stopped at the RED traffic light, waiting to turn onto the Regional Highway. Vehicles zoom by in both directions. The light goes GREEN. Brian signals right and pulls out - SUDDENLY - a big tractor trailer fails to stop at the RED light and SLAMS into the pickup truck on the driver's side. The tractor trailer brakes and the transport wheels lock up and smoke comes off the tires as the trailer jack-knifes. The collision and impact hurls the pickup through the air - the truck smashing, bouncing and rolling across the pavement. Cars, trucks and vans come to a SCREECHING HALT! People quickly exit vehicles and run to assist the crash victims. A tall man in a cowboy hat, a middle-aged lady, and an old couple gather at the mangled red pickup. White engine smoke seeps from the truck's crushed crumpled hood. The 'Good Samaritin' strangers peer in to the truck's passenger cabin - Karen and Brian are severely banged up. The injuries look bad. The two occupants look like contorted rag dolls. A young mother standing with her small child dials 9-1-1.

The Trauma Team at the Hospital's Emergency Department give Brian and Karen Priority 1 medical care. The Doctors and Nurses hover over the devastated couple, each one in their own Hospital gurney. Nurses and ER Technicians attach leads and medical cables. The Doctors examine head and limbs, give injections and check monitor readings. One veteran ER Doctor inspects Brian and quickly announces, "This man has two broken legs, four fractured ribs, and swelling of the brain - We need to induce a Coma!" The other Doctors scan the monitor readings and nod agreement. One Physician goes beside Karen to examine her and remarks, "This woman has a broken leg, a fractured collar bone and a punctured lung! - We'll move her to the O.R." The

Nurses and Orderlies rush to prep Brian and Karen according to the instructions. The team of Doctors set up the procedure to induce Brian into a Coma. Brian's body lays motionless in the Emergency Room. Meanwhile, a Nurse and an Orderly push Karen out of the Emergency Room through a set of double sliding glass doors toward the Operating Room.

Once inside the O.R., the Nurse, Orderly and O.R. Technician transfer Karen's body onto the stainless steel Operating Table that's been prepped and covered with green O.R. sheets. As Karen lays still and serene, O.R. Staff have covered her body with the green medical fabric, only exposing bare skin for the area to be operated on. Nearby, a Surgeon stands ready with O.R. gloves pulled up to his elbows, wearing a surgical cap and mask, an O.R. body suit and protective shoe covering. Medical Technicians attach monitor leads and O.R. Nurses set up the needles for the I.V. and the Anaesthetic. The Surgeon steps up beside the Operating Table and reaches his hand to grab a concave overhead lamp and lowers it for better lighting. He looks at the stainless steel trolly arrayed with surgical scalpels, clamps and pliers, that's been positioned beside him. Two O.R. Nurses dressed in protective medical attire, one beside the Surgeon and the other directly across the O.R. table, stand ready to assist in the Operation. The Surgeon selects a razor sharp scalpel, and extends his arm to hold the tip of the scalpel a couple inches above Karen's exposed skin. The Surgeon looks at Karen out under the Anaesthetic, then he closely focuses on where he will make the incision and calmly remarks, "Okay everybody! Let's help this woman get better!"

# CHAPTER EIGHTEEN

*Searching The Pottery Towns*

It's mid-morning, as Jody and Kei ride the Regional Bus, as it enters the Saga Region that's located in the South West area of Japan. The Bus travels toward the pottery town of **ARITA**. Heading to the town's centre, the Bus passes over one of Arita's bridges decorated with ceramic designs. As the vehicle reaches the middle of town, Jody and Kei look out the window to notice the various SIGNS and BANNERS that advertise the different Pottery Shops located in the community. When the Bus stops, Jody and Kei exit their vehicle to stand beside the roadway. Jody holds up the Shinobi's uncle's ceramic bowl and remarks, "The Map says the Saga Region begins here. Let's start our search, then move to the other towns." Kei nods and comments, "We'll look for this bowl pattern and ask the Potters if they know the artist!" The duo begin to walk toward the Pottery Shops that pepper the street ahead. At the first Shop, Kei and Jody show the small bowl to the lady Potter and she shakes her head - No! In another Shop, Kei bows and talks with an elderly man who waves his hand indicating he doesn't know. Further up the road, a middle-aged Potter holds and examines the bowl, only to shake his head - No! Throughout the morning and into the afternoon, Kei and Jody visit Pottery Shops on various streets, searching for clues and answers. At one location, Kei shows the bowl to a husband and wife Pottery team - they both don't know anything!

On the Bus again, Jody and Kei travel to **IMARI**, a Pottery Town known for its artists producing a distinctive blue ceramic vase. Reaching the town's Pottery section, Jody and Kei look through Shop shelves displaying local ceramic wares. Kei talks with an old man, someone that exhibits years of craft experience - alas, the man shakes his head No! In one Shop, Jody finds a small bowl but it doesn't match the Shinobi Potter's unique style. Once again, as they experienced in ARITA, Jody and Kei go in and out of various Shops but find nothing! Calling it quits for the time being, Jody and Kei walk to a street bench and sit down. The two friends are exhausted and - somewhat dejected! Jody exchanges eye contact with Kei and remarks, "We have to keep looking!" Kei stretches out his legs and replies, "None of these towns have an artist with this style!" Jody turns to face her buddy and comments, "Someone has to recognize the bowl, somewhere! (Pause) What's left?" Kei leans back, takes a breath and replies, "YOBUKO. It's a fishing town - but many artists have shops there." Jody stands to her feet, adjusts her backpack and motions with her arm, "Come on! We have to keep going!" Kei gets to his feet and they walk over to the Regional Bus Zone.

On the Bus yet again, Jody and Kei sit in the front section of the seats and watch the lovely landscape as the vehicle motors along the Highway. After a while, the Bus brings its passengers into the quaint picturesque fishing town of YOBUKO. The Driver steers the Bus through the hamlet's tiny streets until it stops at the Passenger Zone near the fishing wharfs. The Yobuko Harbour is filled with various fishing boats. As Jody and Kei exit the vehicle and move off to the side, SEAGULL CRIES, catch their attention. The two look to see a flock of seagulls flutter above a fishing boat at the Dock as men manoeuvre a net full of fish to offload their catch. Jody and Kei scan the surroundings, and Kei points to a side street with various Banners that belong to Pottery Shops, he exclaims. "Look! A row of Pottery Shops!" Jody replies. "This is the last place - I sure hope he's here!" The duo walk up the pavers toward the first Banner and enter the shop. They are greeted with smiles and bows from a middle-aged husband and wife. The man remarks, "Welcome to our shop! Please look around at our work." The wife adds in, "Our pottery depicts the beautiful ocean." Jody touches Kei's arm and she brings out the small ceramic bowl. Jody comments, "Maybe they will recognize who makes this bowl?" Kei takes the bowl from Jody and presents it to the couple, and enquires, "We seek the artist who makes bowls like this one!" The man clasps the bowl and shows it to his wife. The couple study the bowl - turning it over in their hands to closely inspect the ceramic style. Then the man hands the bowl back to Kei, and remarks, "I've only seen this style once - an old artist used this pattern (Pause) But we've not seen him in a long time." The wife looks at Kei and shakes her head. Kei looks at Jody - who hangs in expectation. He gives her the bowl and comments, "They say an old man used this style - but it was a long time ago!" Jody lowers her gaze to the floor, ponders a second, then suggests, "Ask if they know where he might be?" Kei nods and turns to the couple, "Do you know where he is? - where is his shop?" The man puts his fingertips on his chin and thinks a bit, then his eyes light up and he responds, "There is an artist Co-operative at the town's big wharf. Many artists use it as they tour to sell their ceramic wares. Perhaps he's there!" The man bows after his remark and Kei bows in return, "Uncle. Thank you very much for your help!" Kei turns to Jody and motions her to leave. She eyes Kei and asks, "What did you find out? Is he here?"

As they step out of the shop onto the pavers, Kei looks over at the big wooden wharf at the end of the street. He points and comments, "The Shinobi artist may be at the Co-operative near the wharf. Potters come and go - travelling about selling their work." Jody gives a SIGH and puffs a strand of hair off her face, "Let's go check - I hope he's there. I'm getting tired of all this searching around!" Jody and Kei walk down the street toward the big wharf with its groups of men working their nets and fishing boats.

# CHAPTER NINETEEN

*The Hidden Message*

The Artist Cooperative occupies a large open-air timber shed that has a metal roof to protect from the rains, yet, lets the sea breeze freely flow throughout the vast structure. Underneath the galvanized roof, numerous artists have stalls that display their ceramic work for sale. The entire layout and design resembles a large open-air market, however, instead of vegetables, these artists and vendors sell pottery.

Kei and Jody enter the long wide structure and start to meander through the rows of stalls, checking the various pottery styles. They tread down one row and up another - they have no results! The two stop beside a thick timber post, and Kei comments, "I don't see anything! (Shakes head) All this pottery - and nothing!" Jody slings off her backpack to take out the small bowl. She brings it up eye-level to focus and study it - she looks intently at the blue waves and the swirling white clouds. Still holding the bowl eye-level, she gazes to the right and suddenly notices the very same bowl on a nearby shelf. Jody points and exclaims excitedly, "They're here! The bowls - are here!" Kei spins around and they both stare at the stall across from them. The stall shelves display the very same bowls in different sizes. An elderly man sits relaxed on a wooden stool. Jody and Kei step into the stall and bow before the old man. Kei presents the small bowl to the man, and his eyes light up! Kei politely enquires, "Grandfather, is this bowl your pottery style? Are you the elderly uncle of the village woman in the Iga Mountains?" The old man looks into Kei's eyes, smiles and nods. The aged artist clasps the bowl and gives a quick inspection, then returns it to Kei, and remarks, "The bowl is mine and bears my artist style! - It has my tiny Kanji! (Pause) Examine the clouds." Kei cradles the bowl and slowly turns it over and over as he examines the clouds - then, Kei smiles as his eyes spot the small hidden Kanji for the Japanese word - Mountains! He passes the bowl over to Jody and remarks, "Look carefully at the cloud pattern.(Points) You'll see a hidden Kanji for mountains!" Jody scrutinizes the bowl's design - turning it over in her hand, her eyes tracing the swirling cloud pattern - until - Jody's eyes get wide, "I see it! - a faint Kanji! hidden in the clouds!" Kei and Jody look at the old man and he smiles and nods. Kei bends down eye-level and asks the elderly artist, "Grandfather - do you belong to the Shinobi Ninja Clan?" The old man is suddenly surprised. He glances around and uses his index finger for Kei to come closer. The old man leans forward and quietly remarks, "I am Shinobi but not a Ninja! - I took the Pottery path. (Pause) My older brother is Shinobi Ninja!" Kei responds with excitement, "Where can we find your brother? Is he here in the Saga Region?" The aged artist diverts his eyes to Jody - then back to Kei, and replies, "My brother is in the Tokyo area. I have not seen him for many years. You can look for him there (Pause) Ask for the Beautiful Artist!" Kei taps Jody and motions to stand up. Kei looks at the old man and bows low, Jody does the same. Kei remarks, "Grandfather, Thank you for answering our questions and helping with our search!? The old man's eyes twinkle and he nods with a smile. Jody and Kei turn to leave the stall.

SUDDENLY - the Koroshi-ya springs out from behind the wall holding a red Katana sword. The killer, dressed in a black suit - lifts the blade, points at Jody and demands in broken-English. "American girl - You go Tokyo!" The Koroshi-ya extends his other arm to beckon with an open hand. Kei and the old man instinctively back away toward the rear of the stall. Kei glances and notices there's a service door nearby. Jody scans the stall shelves packed with various bowls of the old man's style. She returns her focus to the professional killer, shakes her head and cries out, "No! NO! - Leave me alone!" The Assassin becomes red-faced in anger and he yells, "American girl - you die! YOU DIE!" The killer lunges forth and swings the sword at Jody. She swiftly tilts to avoid the blade - then quickly steps backward. Jody sees a wooden bucket on the floor closeby - she grabs the handle and brings the bucket in front of her. The killer chops the blade downward from a high angle and Jody swings the bucket to block and deflect the sword. The man counters with a slice at her torso - Jody twirls the bucket to block the strike. She backs up again - now, she's halfway into the confines of the stall. Kei and the old man cower in fear. The Assassin creeps closer with the sharp sword blade pointed level at Jody. He thrusts the blade at Jody's midsection, and Jody pivots to deliver a powerful roundhouse that blasts the man into the wall of pottery shelves. BANG! CRASH! The stall shelves fall apart. The ceramic bowls fall to hit the floor and break into jagged pottery pieces. The Koroshi-ya regains his footing and swings wildly and Jody ducks each sword slice. The man spins the blade and it slices Jody's right shoulder. She grabs the wound - blood seeps down her arm. Jody locks eyes with her attacker. He YELLS and swings the Katana blade with all his might - WHOOSH! Jody tilts her head back and the sword narrowly misses her face - and embeds deeply into the thick timber post beside her. The man struggles to pry the sword free - it's stuck! Jody kicks the man in the groin and he buckles in pain. He reaches out his arm and grabs Jody. She quickly scoops up a large jagged piece of pottery and swipes hard across the man's face and leaves a deep gash. The killer grabs his face and SCREAMS in agony. Jody turns about and leaps high in the air and comes down on the embedded blade with all her weight - the force snaps the blade in half. Kei calls out to Jody - he has the Service Door open and waves to her, "Jody! Hurry! Escape!" Jody dashes for the open door and once she's through, Kei SLAMS the door shut and locks it! In the stall, the killer is bent over clutching his face. He stands upright and notices the Katana handle amid the broken pottery of the ground. He kicks the floor spraying shattered pieces of pottery across the stall. The Koroshi-ya stares at the broken blade embedded in the post - filled with rage and venom - the Koroshi-ya YELLS OUT, "Kisho Kiri Karasu Gaijin!" The Assassin makes a VOW - to kill off the Gaijin!

# CHAPTER TWENTY

*Mending a Wounded Warrior*

Kei and the old potter stand by and watch as an aged fisherman applies the healing arts of Acupuncture and Cupping to Jody. She lays unconscious as numerous Acupuncture needles stick into her skin and cover her body. The old fisherman places and removes glass cups on Jody's back and shoulder. Not far away, a clay pot, a bundle of assorted herbs, and a cup of dark liquid, sit on the worn wooden table nearby. Kei looks at his friend and remarks, "When will she be better?" As he continues to help Jody, the aged fisherman replies, "In three days - the wound will heal and she will be strong enough to travel." Kei and the old potter exchange glances. Kei asks the aged potter, "How will we find your brother?" The old man responds, "I know only what's been told. People in the Tokyo Arts Community know of him as the Beautiful Artist!" Kei studies the old man for a second and comments, "Tokyo is a vast city! What Art Community is he with?" The elderly artist shakes his head with a sad expression and replies, "Young brother, I have no idea! (Pause) You may need to check them all - Fashion Designers, Musicians, Actors, Calligraphers, Tattoo Artists, Painters, - even Sculptors!" Kei looks at Jody laying motionless, he turns to the stone fireplace and stares at the dancing flames of the crackling fire.

THREE DAYS LATER.....

Kei and Jody are onboard the north bound Shinkansen as it speeds toward Tokyo. As the outlaying area and the outskirts of Tokyo come into view, Kei leans over to his friend and remarks, "Soon, we begin the final phase of our quest! Jody stares out the window as the buildings and cityscape zip by. She leans back in her seat and momentarily closes her eyes - She pictures the sparse semi-desert Indian Reservation of Venture. She imagines Her mom, dad and her around the family table. Lastly Jody recalls how Grandpa Carl passes the Golden Seal into her hands. Jody comes out of her daydream and remarks to Kei, "I'm glad you're with me - Tokyo is kinda your city! You're gonna have to take us to the various spots!" Kei smiles and nods, "I'm a Harakuju Hipster (Grins) You're right! Tokyo is my city!" He leans back in his seat and closes his eyes - and unexpectantly begins to SNORE - Jody grins and quietly giggles.

# CHAPTER TWENTY-ONE
*Quest Through Tokyo City*

Kei and Jody exit the Bullet Train and walk the Station Platform mixing with the busy crowd of passengers. The duo exit the doors of the Shinjuku Station onto the busy boulevard full of pedestrian traffic. Tokyo is a mega city with millions of inhabitants, the city streets and transit are always full because people are everywhere. Jody spots a street planter with a bench and motions Kei toward the quieter setting. As the two sit down, Jody asks, "Kei, I need to use your phone. (Pause) I better call to update my mom and dad on what's happening." Kei nods and hands his phone to Jody as she pulls out the International Calling Card and dials home. HOME NUMBER RINGS. Jody looks at Kei and dials again. HOME PHONE RINGS. A serious expression comes over Jody's face as she hands the phone back. Kei sees Jody's worried countenance and asks, "What's wrong?" Jody lifts her eyes to Kei and replies, "No answer! - It's not like my parents to not pick up. Now I'm worried!" Kei reassures his friend, 'I'm sure there's a good explanation. Hey, you'll get through next time!" Jody gives a hopeful smile and the two get off the bench to resume their trek down the busy street. As they walk, Jody looks at Kei and remarks, "You said you have a friend in the Entertainment District. Will he be able to help?" Kei replies as he strides along, "Koji works at a popular Night Club. He's connected and knows lots of people.' Jody quickens her pace and replies, "Well! - Let's get started!" They move along with the pedestrian traffic.

It's night time in Tokyo's Entertainment District. Inside the Night Club where Koji works, young people pack the dance floor as the animated DJ pumps the EDM to blast out the music. Coloured lights and lasers illuminate the Club's space. Groups of patrons party at tables with lounge chairs that surround the Club's neon-lit interior. Jody and Kei are at the front of a line inside the Club's front lobby. Kei talks with a Security Staff who's fitted with a communication headset. Kei tells the guy, "I want to talk with my friend Koji! He works here." The guy turns his head to look into the Club's interior - then waves to beckon with his hand. The Club's hallway soon fills with the massive body of a huge Security guy. The big brute strides toward Jody and Kei - then breaks out with a huge smile, and remarks, "Kei, old friend, so good to see you. (Pause) Do you want to get into the Club?" The big friend manhandles Kei in a friendly way, as Kei attempts to fend off the playful action. Kei looks at his childhood buddy and asks, "Koji, pal - I'm with this Gaijin girl. We need to ask you something important!" Koji glances at Jody, then scans the lobby and gestures to gather in a side cove and comments, "Let's go over there. I'm on duty so I can't talk long." The trio walk across the lobby and huddle in the room's cove, away from the line of patrons and Security Staff. Kei looks up at his big friend, "You've worked the Entertainment world for many years. My Gaijin friend, Jody, needs to find someone called the Beautiful Artist. - Have you ever heard that name before?" Koji ponders a few seconds, then puts his hand on Kei's shoulder and replies, "I've met lots of Celebrities, Performers and Artists, but I don't know this Beautiful Artist!" Kei exclaims, "Koji, if you don't know - how will we find out?" The large guy looks at Kei and Jody and replies, "Someone in Tokyo's art world is bound to know who you're looking for. - Keep searching!" The big guy turns and walks away to disappear into the Club's neon-lit hallway. Jody tugs on Kei's arm and asks, "What did you find out?" Kei responds, "My friend doesn't know - but he said we have to keep looking!" Jody gets a big frown. The two exit the Club's lobby doors.

Kei and Jody encounter Tokyo's night life as they continue to search venues and seek answers. At a Paint Studio, Jody and Kei talk with two artists that indicate no knowledge. In an alleyway at a Theatre Backstage door, Kei questions an Actress, and she doesn't know. Jody stands to the side and watches as Kei talks with some Fashion Models - they reply NO! Later on, Jody and Kei sit with an old Sculptor - he shakes his head NO! The duo enter a shop that sells lovely Japanese Dolls - they leave shortly with no success. At one point during the evening, Kei and Jody speak with a Lady Calligrapher, but she has never heard of such a person. As Jody and Kei walk along, they notice a street lined with Tattoo Parlours. They lock up at an overhead Banner that features a Dragon amid Cherry Blossoms. Jody turns to Kei, "Let's try here!" Kei grabs the handle and pushes the front door open.

The Tattoo Parlour walls are covered with colourful vivid drawings of Koi Fish, Cherry Blossoms, Samurai Warriors, Galloping Horses, Bamboo Forests, and Fierce Dragons. The Studio interior features stone carvings, vases of beautiful flowers, and lovely Bonsai trees on display stands. Jody and Kei step into the golden glow of the Tattoo Parlour. They move to the middle of the shop and look about. Out from a beaded curtain, steps an elderly Tattoo Artist, who politely bows and greets them, "Welcome to my humble studio!" Kei and Jody bow respect, and Kei asks, "Grandfather, we look for someone that you might know." The old man moves to sit on a carved teak bench and replies, "Who is it that you seek?" Kei responds, "Do you know someone called the Beautiful Artist?" The old man's eyes twinkle as he smiles wide. He stands up and walks over to stand before a watercolour painting of a Samurai Warrior, and comments, "The one you seek is indeed a Beautiful Artist. I've known him for a long time!" Kei turns to Jody with excitement, 'He knows who we're looking for!" Jody's eyes grow wide - she's thrilled at the news. Kei looks at the Tattoo Artist and remarks, "Kindly tell us where we can find this person?" The man moves to a large stunning Bonsai tree that sits on a table and he touches the branches with care and respect. The elderly artist gazes at Kei and Jody as he rests his fingers on the elegant time-sculpted trunk of the Bonsai tree and replies, "The man you seek - gave me this outstanding Bonsai tree many years ago! (Eyes Bonsai) Wonderful isn't it? (Pause) We call him the Beautiful Artist because he nurtures and shapes these beautiful bonsai." Kei turns to Jody, "The one we look (Points) gave him that Bonsai tree!" Jody looks at the Bonsai and old man with an exuberant gaze. Kei shifts his eyes to the aged tattoo artist and asks, "Where can we find him? It is very important!" The old man comes up to them and responds, "He owns a Bonsai Nursery on the outskirts of North Tokyo! - The Nursery Banner has a Bonsai over the Kanji for Sword. The Nursery borders a protected forest area." Kei bows very low to the elderly man - who bows in return, and Kei remarks, "Grandfather, our deepest gratitude for your help!" Kei looks at Jody and motions for them to leave. Jody bows to the elderly man and accompanies Kei toward the front door.

The old Tattoo Artist watches them as they leave the Tattoo Parlour. On the side walk outside, Jody tugs on Kei's arm, "Where do we go next?" Kei glances at Jody and remarks, "The outskirts of North Tokyo. We look for a Bonsai Nursery!" Jody and Kei walk down the street past a Noodle Bar.

A couple of Hanzai-shu thugs are inside and the two gangsters recognize Jody. One thug quickly pulls out his cell phone to call. At the Hanzai-shu Headquarters, gang members cluster in different groups, some smoke cigarettes and talk, others drink and play cards - while some peruse magazines, and others simply chill out. The Hanzai-shu Leader's cell phone BUZZES - and he picks up to hear the voice of one of his henchmen, "Boss. We saw that Gaijin girl - she's near the Tattoo Shops." The Gang Leader sneers and orders, "Good! Follow her - but stay out of sight. Let me know where they go." At the Noodle Bar, the thug bows as he holds his phone, "Hai!"

# CHAPTER TWENTY-TWO
### *Bonsai Over Sword*

On the northern outskirts of Tokyo City, the rural countryside basks in the warmth of the morning sun. A gentle wind blows through the trees and the leaves rustle in the breeze. Birds on forest branches chirp their songs into the air. The sky above is a light clear blue.

A Transit Bus drives the country road and brakes at a rural Bus Stop. Jody and Kei step off the Bus into the roadside gravel. the Bus signals and proceeds down the road. A short distance down the road is a tall post with a Banner that flutters in the gentle breeze. Jody and Kei walk toward the weathered wood post, stop and look up at the white Banner that features a black Bonsai over a red Kanji for Sword. Kei and Jody begin to move over the tarmac toward the large wooden gate of the Nursery entrance. Jody remarks to Kei, "I'm feeling nervous to finally meet him - just think! - the last member of the Ninja Clan!" Kei watches his friend and comments, "You have flown from America - travelled Japan - fought Japanese gangsters and searched hard - Now! - You complete your quest!" They both turn and face the Nursery entrance and Kei pushes the heavy timber gate open. Before them is an oriental pathway that goes under a large red Japanese Tori Gate, then leads toward a wide open area of fields and trees. Passing beneath the Red Tori Gate, Jody and Kei tread along the manicured garden pathway until they come to an open area with rows of wooden tables. A potted Bonsai sits on each table. Jody and Kei look around and see wood buildings that line the ground's perimeter. The Bonsai Nursery is clean and tidy, simple and refined. Off to the side, a Bonsai worker dressed in plain tunic and trousers, exits a building close by. He approaches them and bows low, "Welcome strangers! How may we help you?" Kei glances at Jody, then he looks at the worker and remarks, "We seek the one called the Beautiful Artist! My Gaijin friend has something very important for him." The worker's eyes get wide and his eye brows raise. He quickly turns and hastens to the large central wood building and enters inside. Within seconds, an elderly man with white hair braided in a ponytail, accompanied by several workers, exits the structure and make their way toward Jody and Kei. The elderly man is dressed in a simple plain tunic and trousers. He stops a few feet from Jody and Kei - Kei and Jody bow low in respect to him. The man comments, "I am known as the Beautiful Artist! My worker tells me that you wish to speak with me?" Kei looks at the aged man and remarks, "Grandfather, my Gaijin friend, Jody, carries a special gift for you!" Kei lifts himself upright and extends his arm to Jody. The elderly man turns his gaze to Jody and smiles. Jody straightens up and reaches into her backpack to bring out the cloth wrapped item. She respectfully approaches the old man and puts out her arm. The old man takes the wrapped bundle and holds it in his open palm. He carefully unfolds the cloth to reveal the object. The Beautiful Artist's eyes grow wide, his eye brows arch, his mouth drops open - he's totally awestruck! **THE GOLDEN SEAL!** The old man turns the Golden Seal over and over in his hand - to closely examine the engravings and details. With jubilation, he holds it up for the gathered Nursery workers to see. The workers murmur with excitement! The old man stares at Jody for a few moments, then he asks, "Where did you find the long lost Golden Seal?" Kei steps forward and bows low to explain, "Grandfather, my Gaijin friend, Jody, carried the Golden Seal from her home in America, to deliver it to you - the last of the Shinobi Ninja Clan. (Pause) My friend has fought and defeated Hanzai-shu thugs to return this special gift to you!" The Beautiful Artist's eyes become moist - he is choked up with emotion. The old man steps softly to stand before Jody - Jody bows low and holds her position. The Beautiful Artist has a tender smile and he places his hand under Jody's chin to gently coax her upright. Jody straightens up. The elderly man looks at Kei and points to Jody and remarks, "Your Gaijin friend - Jody - is a true warrior! The Shinobi Ninja Clan is indebted to her for bringing us the **GORUDOSHIRU - our Golden Seal!**" The old leader turns and beckons to an aid close by and whispers into the his ear. The aid quickly bows and runs off to the large central wood building. Within a few minutes, the aid returns to hand a black velvet pouch to the elderly leader. The old man opens the pouch, turns to Jody and extends his hand - and looks at Kei, who remarks to Jody, "I think he wants to give you something!" Jody opens her hand and the Beautiful Artist lays an engraved thick gold medallion on Jody's palm. Jody's eyes zoom large. The old man remarks, "I give your Gaijin friend - the **SHOCHO TUKEN -** a special Ninja Token only given to the **IDAINA SENSHI -** a Great Warrior! It is our humble way to say Thank You for returning the Golden Seal!" Jody stares at the glistening gold object. Kei steps beside her to explain, "The Shinobi Ninja Master has given you a great honour! This Gold Token is only given to a Great Warrior! - He wants you to have it!" Jody looks at the elderly Ninja Master and bows low, and comments, "Okini Arigato!" The Beautiful Artist smiles deeply and nods acknowledgement.

**SUDDENLY!**

The Koroshi-ya and the Hanzai-shu Leader step out from around a building, each holding a Katana sword. The Gang Leader YELLS, "Attack! Wipe them out!" Thugs with swords, axes, knives and clubs, pour out from bushes, trees and buildings toward Jody, Kei, and the gathered Nursery workers. The Hanzai-shu Leader and the Koroshi-ya run directly at Jody and Kei. Jody steps in front of Kei to protect him. The Beautiful Artist, the Ninja Master, grabs a bamboo pole to defend. The old Ninja Master looks at his Nursery workers and instructs, "Defend - but do not kill any!" All the Bonsai workers, who are secretly skilled Ninjas, swiftly grab shovels, rakes, wood poles, and garden tools for weapons.

The Hanzai-shu thugs and the Ninja - CLASH!

Thugs swing swords, swipe knives and flail clubs at the Bonsai workers, who unleash their Ninja fighting skills! One thug swings his blade and the Ninja ducks, summersaults forward to kick the hoodlum unconscious. Another gangster repeatedly jabs his knife at a Nursery worker, who spins around to grab the thug's hand to disarm. The Nursery worker pummels the gangster to knock him out! The Hanzai-shu Leader raises his Katana, and with two henchmen with long knives - attack the old Ninja Master from three sides. The Gang Leader and the two thugs swing their weapons. The aged Ninja Master skillfully dodges the sharp blades, and twirls the bamboo pole to knock out both henchmen. Now, just the Hanzai-shu Leader and the old Ninja Master face each other! As the two men confront each other, all around them, the Ninja Bonsai workers decimate the street thugs with a barrage of kicks, powerful strikes and devastating blows. The hoodlums lay across the Nursery grounds - injured, defeated and unconscious. The Gang Leader and the Beautiful Artist circle each other, the Gang Leader boasts, "The Koroshi-ya told us about the Golden Seal - and the secret treasure!" The Beautiful Artist replies in a determined voice, "The treasure belongs to the Shinobi Ninja Clan! You will not get it!" The Gang Leader thrusts his sword blade repeatedly as he moves about - the old man moves the pole to flick the blade away each time.

Off to the side not far away...

The Koroshi-ya, who is extremely angry, twirls his sword before Jody who is unarmed. The professional killer boldly states, "You die American girl! - I kill - You die now!" Jody keenly watches as the killer paces back and forth in front of her. He sweeps the razor sharp blade from side to side. Jody crouches slightly with both arms extended for battle. She quickly glances at a nearby table with a large Bonsai. The Koroshi-ya lunges the sword to attack. Jody swiftly pivots and dashes toward the nearby table, the killer racing after her with the sword pointed at Jody's back. Jody runs and stretches out to grab the thick branches of the Bonsai tree. Her fingers hook the top branches and she spins about to kick away the oncoming sword. She powerfully swings the potted Bonsai tree at the killer's head. CRASH! The Bonsai's stone planter smashes into the killer's head - the stone basin cracks and splits apart and loose dirt falls - the Koroshi-ya's eyes roll as he's knocked out and drops to the ground! Jody stares at the fallen killer as she catches her breath. Now, all eyes are on the Hanzai-shu Leader and the old Ninja Master. The Gang Leader scans around to see thugs scattered about - unconscious, injured or surrendered. The Beautiful Artist remarks, "Your gang is defeated - Give up!" The Hanzai-shu Leader smirks - then raises his Katana sword and cries out, "Never! - I will kill you instead!" The Gang Leader wildly swings the Katana blade - the old man deftly ducks and dodges each attack. As the Gang Leader lunges to skewer the old man, the Ninja Master stops him with a mighty blow! The aged Ninja Master quickly strikes the gangster in several places all over his body - then the old man steps away. The hoodlum is locked - unable to move a muscle whatever - he's frozen like a statue! The Beautiful Artist remarks, "There! You will stay this way until I release you." The Hanzai-shu Leader bellows, "Old man, what did you do? (Straining. Grunting) I can't move! Can not move!" The Ninja Master replies, "I simply locked you up until the Police arrive to officially lock you up!" The Ninja Master glances at his Nursery workers and makes a quick gesture. The Bonsai Ninja gather all the gangsters together and tie them up for the Police. The Bonsai Ninja fashion intricate rope bonds to hold and secure all the Hanzai-shu. Jody approaches the Beautiful Artist, and Kei steps out from amid the Nursery workers to join Jody. She bows low before the old man and comments, "Thank you for saving me from those gangsters! Okini Arigato!" The elderly warrior gives Jody a tender smile. He reaches into his tunic and brings out his hand to display the Golden Seal. He speaks in broken-English, "Jody - you - Ninja! (Points) Ninja!" Jody's eyes light up - she grins wide. Kei is gobsmacked! Jody looks at the Beautiful Artist, scans the Nursery grounds and all the lovely Bonsai trees, then turns toward Kei, "I did it! - completed my Grandfather's dying request and returned the Golden Seal! (Pause) Now, I must return home." Her good friend remarks, "I'll go with you to the Airport. After all, your Japanese isn't that good - you need me!" Jody with a twinkle in her eye, replies, "That's right - you're a good translator - and a pretty good friend." Kei smiles. As the duo turn to leave the Nursery grounds and walk down the path, they turn and wave to the Beautiful Artist and the Bonsai workers, who wave back in return. With Kei and Jody well down the path toward the front gate, the Ninja Master grips the Golden Seal in his hand and raises it in Victory!. All the Bonsai Ninja rally around  - and CELEBRATE!

# CHAPTER TWENTY-THREE

*Flying Home*

Kei is with Jody outside the International Departure lounge at the Narita Airport that's located on the outskirts of metropolitan Tokyo. Travellers and tourists mill about the busy interior of the Terminal. Individuals and families steer luggage trollies here and there toward various Airport Gates. Jody stands next to her luggage trolly and she shifts her backpack to be more comfortable. She holds her Boarding Pass and gives Kei a tender gaze, "I don't know how to thank you for all your help! - I couldn't have done it without you!" Kei smiles in a sheepish manner and replies, "I was honoured to assist you - not every Japanese guy gets to fulfill Bushido these days! (Grins) Very cool!" Jody gives Kei an offer, "If you ever get to the States - look me up! You got my address." Kei tilts his head with a smile, "America is a long way from Japan! (Laughs) Maybe, I'll visit when I'm old and have enough money." Jody looks wistfully at her friend and leans forward to give a quick kiss on Kei's cheek, "You're welcome to visit anytime! Call me - you have my number." Kei nods and Jody moves her trolly toward the Departure Zone entrance - the frosted glass doors slide open to give access. Jody looks at Kei one final time, gives a big wave and walks through into Departures - and the glass doors close. As she makes her way, Jody notices an Airport Pay Phone Kiosk.


Jody walks up to the Kiosk and grabs the phone handle, swipes the credit card and dials home. She listens to the ELECTRONIC TONES then her mom's voice on the Answering Machine, "We can't come to the phone right now. Please leave your message after the tone - BEEP!" Jody blurts out, "Mom. Dad. I've been trying to reach you! I heading home. See you guys soon, ok. Love Ya! Bye." Jody hangs up the phone receiver and moves her trolly toward the Boarding Zone. She joins some other passengers who are lined up in front of the United Airlines Boarding Desk, where Airline Staff check Boarding Passes. Just beyond the Boarding Desk is the enclosed Gangway that leads to the aircraft. After her Boarding Pass for United Airlines Flight 252 is checked and her trolly tagged for loading, Jody walks with other travellers on the Gangway toward the plane's open doors where the Stewardesses greet and direct them. Jody shuffles down the cabin aisle to her row, stores the backpack into the overhead compartment, sits down and tucks the carry-on under her seat. She sits in her window seat that's situated a few rows ahead of the plane's wing. The seat beside her stays empty as a middle-aged businessman settles into the aisle seat. Jody glances around as passengers clog the aisles as they find their seats and hoist their luggage into the overhead bins. **CHIMES. SEAT BELT LIGHT.** Passengers quickly get seated and start to buckle up. The Stewardesses position at the front of cabin sections and start to give Flight Instructions. **AIRCRAFT ENGINES HIGH PITCH WHIRL!** The plane begins to roll forward, taxis and positions on the Airport tarmac. The big engines **THROTTLE. VROOM!** and the plane quickly picks up speed on the runway and the velocity pushes Jody back in her seat. She glances around as the plane's interior vibrates. This time - Jody is relaxed and calm! The plane reaches Lift-Off and the shaking stops. The aircraft climbs at a steep angle - then it levels off. **SEAT BELT LIGHT OFF**. Jody looks out her window at the wonderful Japanese landscape below. Hours later, the aircraft flies the clear night sky where bright stars fill the heavens. Inside the Pilot's cockpit, the Altitude Gage reads - 30,000 feet. As the plane heads over the Pacific Ocean - Jody's seat is reclined as she sleeps peacefully curled up in a blanket.

Near dawn, the Aircraft lands safely on the runway flanked by coloured navigation lights on the grounds of Sweetwater County Airport. The plane taxis to the Terminal as an Airport worker waves lit batons to guide the pilots to dock with the extended Gangway. Jody exits the Passenger Gangway and walks through the Airport to retrieve her trolly, then she goes through the Terminal Exit Doors. Taxis are parked out front and she gets a cab. As the driver stores the trolly in the trunk, Jody gets into the back seat. The driver gets behind the steering wheel and looks at Jody, who remarks, "1580 Plains Road, Venture Indian Reservation." The driver nods, enters info on the GPS, starts the engine and the cab's meter - then, the cab drives away from the Terminal. As the Taxi Cab rolls along, Jody looks out at the city lights of Rock Springs, Wyoming. As the morning sun breaks the horizon, the taxi passes over the Highway until coming to the rural tarmac roads of the Indian Reservation. The Driver turns onto the Concession with the sign that reads - **PLAINS ROAD**. Jody stares out the back window at the semi-desert terrain The taxi approaches a raised ranch bungalow up on the right. The roadside mailbox - **LONG GRASS**. The taxi turns into the laneway and parks. The driver exits the car and gets the trolly out of the trunk and sets it on the grass. Jody gets out of the car and hands the driver the proper fare plus a generous tip. The Driver nods appreciation, gets into his car and drives off.

In the morning light, Jody stares at the the house - curtains drawn and no sign of life. She grabs her trolly and carries it to the front cement step, inserts and turns her house key and opens the door wide. Jody happily yells out, "Hello! Mom. Dad. I'm home!" **SILENCE**. Jody lifts the trolly inside and sets it near the front window - then closes the door. She quickly walks around the house - peers in the kitchen, looks in her parent's bedroom, the backroom - Nothing! Jody's greatly puzzled?! She sits bewildered at the dining table, and goes to the home phone beside the sofa - and dials the RESERVATION POLICE. ELECTRONIC DIAL TONES. An Officer picks up, "Hello. Venture Police Station." Jody remarks in a serious tone, "Hi. My name is Jody Long Grass - and my parents are missing! - I can't seem to contact them. It's not like them and I'm worried!" The Officer enquires, "What did you say your name was?" Jody replies, "Jody Long Grass. My parents are Brian and Karen Long Grass. I've been trying to phone them for days - and they're not home!" The Policeman comments, "I'm going to put you on hold as I check our system." Jody replies, "That's okay. I'll hold." TELEPHONE SILENCE. The Reservation Police Officer comes back on the phone and asks, "Hello Jody - do you live on the Indian Reservation at 1580 Plains Road?" Jody quickly responds, "Yes! That's our home address!" There's a few seconds of silence, then the Officer speaks, "Jody. (Pause) I'm afraid I have some bad news for you - Your dad and mom were in a terrible car accident with a tractor trailer. We arrested the truck driver on DUI and running a Red Light - We put him in jail!" (Pause) The reason you weren't able to reach your parents is because your dad and mom are at the Regional Hospital - listed in Critical Condition." Jody is stunned and shocked by the tragic news - she's speechless! The Police Officer voices concern, "Hello Jody!

- Jody you still there?" Jody quietly responds, "Thank you for letting me know! (Pause) I've gotta go now." Jody puts down the phone receiver and stares off for a moment. Suddenly, she dashes over to grab her backpack and rushes out the front door.

# CHAPTER TWENTY-FOUR

*Parents In Critical Care*

Jody walks through the sliding glass doors of the Regional Hospital and enters the modern lobby. She scans around and makes a beeline to the lady Volunteer wearing a smock behind the Information Desk. The kind faced lady looks up and Jody remarks, "Hello! I'm looking for Brian and Karen Long Grass?" The woman types in keystrokes and peers at the monitor screen, "Brian Long Grass is in the Intensive Care Unit. Karen Long Grass is in the Rehab Unit on the 2nd Floor." Jody smiles and comments, "Thank you very much!" Jody turns about and walks to the Lobby Elevators and stands beside a family of four who are waiting. ELEVATOR CHIMES. The elevator door opens and Jody and the family enter inside - and Jody pushes the 2nd Floor button. The elevator reaches the second level, the doors open and Jody steps out into the corridor. Jody moves to the Nursing Station to enquire about her mom's room. A Rehab Nurse guides Jody to the Hospital Room doorway and comments, "Your mother just finished her Rehab session an hour ago - she's pretty tired out." The Nurse turns and leaves. Jody looks at her mom laying in the Hospital bed with her eyes closed. The room has three other patients - their divider curtains are extended for privacy. Jody quietly comes up to her mom's bed. She glances at the blue marks of bruised skin and the tiny lacerations on her mom's face as a result of the accident. A Rehab sling suspends her mom's right leg. Jody bends down close to her mom's face and gently whispers, "Mom. Mom. - It's me, Jody! I'm back." Karen's eye lids flutter and she opens her eyes and looks up with a tired gaze - then smiles wide, "Jody honey, I'm so happy you're here! I was so worried about you." Jody leans in a tender gaze and lovingly stroke her mom's hair, then proudly remarks, "Mom. I did it! I finished what Grandpa asked me to do - returned the Golden Seal!" Karen's eyes wide and a motherly smile covers her face, "Your dad and I are so proud of you! - What you accomplished! (Pause) Did they tell you what happened?" Jody lowers to partially sit on the edge of the bed and replies, "A Reservation Officer gave me the details - that Transport Driver was arrested and charged for DUI and running a Red Light. He's behind bars now! (Pause) The Nurse told me you have six more weeks of Rehab (Pause) and Dad's in a coma!" Karen's eyes well up and tears roll down her face, "I don't know how long Brian will be in a Coma! The doctors are waiting for the brain swelling to do down. (Crying) Jody, I'm so scared we're going to lose him!" Jody leans in with a big hug and squeezes her mom's hand to reassure, "Dad's going to make it! Mom, don't worry, the Doctors will make him better - you'll see!" Karen turns her head toward the window with it's blinds pulled open, "I pray to God every day that Brian will get better. (Tears) I can't bear the thought of living without him!" Jody looks tenderly into her mom's moist eyes, "Soon, you both will be out of here and back home - just like before all this happened. - We'll fish at the Creek, and get ice cream at Emma May's." Karen smiles at her daughter's words, then looks at Jody and remarks, "I want you to call your Aunt Sally and ask her to come stay with you." Jody sits up straight and replies, "Mom, it's okay - I don't need help - you know I can handle myself." The mother replies with a faint smile, "I know you can handle yourself - But you still need company. It would make me feel better!" Jody rolls her eyes slightly then complies, "Alright mom, I'll call Aunt Sally!" Her mom comments, "That's good Jody! Do it for me - I'll feel better knowing someone is there with you." The talk has Karen tired out and her eyes get droopy, she remarks in a fading voice, "Sorry honey, this pain medication - makes me - so tired - I have to close - my eyes." Karen is out. Jody lets go of her mom's hand. She adjusts her mother's pillow and pulls up the bed cover - and leans over to kiss her mom's forehead. Jody leaves the Hospital's Rehab Department, enters the elevator and presses the button for the 5th Floor.

Jody reaches the floor level and enquires at the Nursing Desk about the patient, Brian Long Grass. An ICU Nurse lets Jody into the Intensive Care Unit and guides her to his location. As the Nurse returns to her station, Jody steps up close beside the bed and stares at her father. The rhythmic sounds of the Breathing Apparatus fills the air. Jody scans her dad's motionless form - and sniffles as tears roll down her cheeks. Jody has a momentary flashback to an better - earlier time, to when she and her dad spent the afternoon fishing in a boat on a river. It was a warm lazy wonderful time outdoors together. Jody blinks her eyes and stares down at the I.V. tube, monitor leads, and the breathing apparatus over her dad's nose and mouth. She stands still for a couple moments, then turns to slowly walk away.

A few days later at home - KNOCKS on the front door! Jody gets off the sofa to open the front door to see who it is. Aunt Sally stands on the cement stoop wearing a big smile and holding a small suitcase. Jody greets her aunt with a smile, "Hi Aunt Sally! Come on in - I got your room ready." Aunt Sally, her mom's sister, is a happy plump lady with curly auburn hair and winsome eyes. The lady steps inside, gives a hug and looks Jody over from head to toe, and exclaims, "Jody - my how you've grown!" Jody grins as she replies, 'Last time you saw me - I was in Grade 8." Aunt Sally sets her suitcase down, straightens her blouse and looks at her niece, and compliments, "You were a little girl then - But look at you now! Such a fine young lady!" Jody picks up Sally's suitcase and remarks as she motions to an armchair, "You must be tired from your long trip. I'll take your suitcase to the spare room - you can just relax!" The woman smiles wide, strolls over to the armchair, sits down and begins to preen her permed hairdo. Sally gives a SIGH and remarks, "Must admit - I'm a bit tuckered out from that long taxi ride." Jody smiles, turns and disappears down the hall.

Over the next few weeks, Aunt Sally preps and cooks food in the kitchen. She dusts, sweeps and mops floors and scrubs walls. The lady does the laundry, and Jody helps Sally fold the clean bed sheets. In the evening, Sally sits in the armchair sewing on buttons and crocheting doilies. Jody begins to see the wisdom of her mom's request to have Aunt Sally stay.

One late afternoon, Jody and Aunt Sally eat supper at the dining table - when there's **KNOCKS** at the front door. Aunt Sally opens the door to see who's calling - and looks out to see an elderly American Indian man dressed in a plain black tunic and pants standing before her. The man holds a black envelope. The man politely enquires, "Good Day! Is Jody Long Grass here?" Aunt Sally smiles and replies, "Just a minute please - I'll call her. (Turns her head) Jody. Jody dear - someone's here for you." Jody rises from the dining table and walks to the front door to stand beside her aunt. Jody looks at the man in simple plain attire and informs, "Hello! I'm Jody Long Grass!" The man smiles, bows and straightens up, then hands Jody the black envelope, and remarks, "You are invited to - **Black Eagle**!" Jody's is surprised and shocked, her eyes get big like saucers. She looks down at the black envelope in her hand, and turns it over and touches the red wax seal that bears the Japanese Kanji for - Black Eagle. Jody's fingers slightly tremble as she opens the envelope - she takes out the parchment paper letter and slowly scans it.

## FORMAL INVITATION TO BLACK EAGLE

Jody lifts her eyes to look at the elderly man and remarks with utter joy, "Thank You! Thank You so very much!" The elderly man steps back, bows low, returns upright and remarks, "The Competition starts in 3 weeks. Instructions and directions are included in the letter. (Smiles) Congratulations!" Jody and Aunt Sally watch from the open doorway as the man descends the front stoop, gets into a shiny black sedan with tinted glass, and the car drives away. Aunt Sally glances over at Jody standing still, and asks, "Is it something important?" Jody turns to her and holds up the letter and black envelope, and give an ecstatic reply, "Just the best news ever! (Pause) This is about Black Eagle!" Aunt Sally watches as Jody tears off to her bedroom with excitement and joy. The lady closes the front door and remarks in a whimsical mutter, "Imagine. All this fuss over a bird!"

# CHAPTER TWENTY-FIVE
## Black Eagle

The morning sun breaks across the rugged terrain. Somewhere in the rocky landscape, a cavernous stone amphitheatre with a wide flat centre and stepped elevations, lays secluded in the wilderness. This natural forum carved by time and wind, is this year's location for the authoritative and highly regarded, Ninjan **BLACK EAGLE** - a Tournament held every five years. Participants from various American Indian Tribes are selected and officially invited to the renowned Competition.

Jody stands with assembled guys and gals - each one is an official contestant for Black Eagle. They gather around a tall thick wood post deeply embedded in the centre of the arena's earthen floor. She looks around at her competitors - most are young people in their 20's and 30's. There a few males and females who are a little older. The contestants have mixed emotions, some stand alert and ready, others are chill and relaxed, some are talking. Suddenly, there's the high pitched **SHRILL** - a black whistle arrow strikes the top of the post several feet above the contestants' heads.  All eye rivet to the arrow. Next, the pounding sound of **Indian Drums** fill the air - followed by a loud **Indian War Cry**! Then - **SILENCE**.


Suddenly, The Grand Master and five Black Eagle Judges dressed as Ninjans quickly appear on an upper elevation. The Grand Master holds a golden staff. Jody and the other participants quickly look up. The Grand Master motions his arm and Ninjans appear on a lower level - each raise their weapon specialty high in the air - **Bow and Arrow - Open Hand - Tomahawk - War Club - Spear - Knife - Sword**.

The assembled young people look at the weapon specialists and the Judges. The Grand Master gazes down at the invited contestants and announces, "Welcome to Black Eagle!" Jody and the others swiftly focus on the Grand Master. The elderly Ninjan Master continues his address, "Today, you will be tested through the Fire of Combat! Each of you must prove your Ninjan skills with four weapons. Each one must defeat their opponent to advance to the next round. (Pause) The Winner will be awarded the Tournament Scroll and the Black Eagle Sword. A Judge on the Grand Master's left - lifts up his arm holding the Scroll, the Judge on the Grand Master's right - lifts his arm holding the Black Eagle Katana. The Judge holding the Sword announces, "The Ninjan who displays expert skills and defeats all foes - will received the Tournament Scroll, and be awarded the prized Black Eagle Sword!" The Grand Master steps forward and extends the golden staff out over the group of contestants, and remarks, "We have invited you here from many Indian Tribes. Each contestant will wear their Tribe's Ninjan outfit for the competition. - This is to honour your people and native culture. A Tribal Elder will accompany each of you. (Looks at the group) Now - Let Black Eagle begin!

The Judges and the Ninjans on the lower level disappear from sight. All the contestants look at each other - many are eager and pumped with excitement! Everyone turns their attention to the perimeter of the wide amphitheatre floor; various Tribal Elders dressed in their Tribe's attire beckon with their hands. Each contestant recognizes their Tribe's clothing and heads toward their respective Elder. Jody scans around, to her right is a middle-aged man dressed in traditional Shoshone garb. She walks toward him. As she gets near, the Shoshone Elder smiles and greets her, "Hi Jody! You don't know me - but I was a good friend of your Grandpa Carl. (Pause) Let's go and get you ready for the Competition!" The man escorts Jody to an area where there's an enclosure with opaque black canvass walls and roof covering. The man stops a couple feet before the enclosure entrance and points. Jody comments, "You want me to go inside?" The Tribal Elder responds, "Yes! You will find everything you need - Shoshone Ninjan clothing and various tribal decorations."

Jody glances at the man, nods and smiles, then walks to the entrance and disappears inside. Once inside the tent-like structure that's screened for privacy, Jody sees Shoshone Ninjan clothing on a long wood table. At one end are Tribal trinkets and decorations. At the other end, is a hand mirror, dark towel, and clay bowls filled with different coloured pigment. Jody steps close to the table and surveys her clothing options. After Jody has put together her outfit, she exits the dark canvass shelter and remarks, "Guess I'm ready as I'll ever be!" The Shoshone Elder turns around to face the enclosure entrance. Jody emerges dressed as a Shoshone Ninjan with a red feather in her long hair, and a hair braid on each side with coloured beads and silver disks. War Paint is on her face - red covers her forehead, black is streaked across her eyes from one temple to the other. Jody has applied the War Paint in the style of an experienced Shoshone Warrior! The Elder gives a big smile and comments. "You honour all our Shoshone people - and especially your Grandfather!" Jody smiles at his remark. The Elder motions that she join him. They both walk back to the arena's wide flat earthen floor. Some others contestants have already gathered and stand with their Tribal Elder. Jody and her Elder join them. A few others make their way onto the Tournament floor. Now, every contestant is in their Tribe's Ninjan outfit and war paint.

## DRUMS BEAT

The Grand Master and the Judges assemble on an upper elevation that gives them a clear vantage point for the Competition. The Grand Master lifts his voice to instruct, "Contestants - step forward to form a single line and present yourselves to the Black Eagle Judges!" Each contestant steps out to help form a line across the Combat area. The Grand Master, the Black Eagle Judges, and the Ninjan Masters, fix their eyes on each contestant. All the young people look healthy and strong, fit and capable for Tournament Combat. The Black Eagle Judges gaze at the line of young warriors - they see - a young man standing tall and proud as a **SIOUX** Ninjan, beside him is an older man dressed in **CROW** Ninjan clothing, next in line is a young woman wearing a **CHEYENNE** Ninjan outfit, and to her right is a young man with an **IROQUOIS** Ninjan outfit and haircut. The Judges continue their visual sweep of the Competition entrees. They look at a woman fitted with **LAKOTA** Ninjan garb, next to her is a young man in **APACHE** Ninjan clothing, and beside him is Jody dressed as a **SHOSHONE** Ninjan. The Tournament Officials scan the line further to see an older man standing as a **NAVAJO** Ninjan, then a young lady in her **KIOWA** Ninjan outfit. The remaining contestants include - a young man in **ARAPAHO** Ninjan clothing, an older man dressed as a **BLACKFOOT** Ninjan, and lastly, a young man stands in his **UTE** Ninjan attire. The Grand Master and the Black Eagle Judges nod and bow to show their approval to all the assembled young Ninjans. The Grand Master waves his hand and all the Ninjan Weapon Masters appear - each hold a Tournament weapon high in the air - Bow and Arrow - Open Hand - Tomahawk - War Club - Spear - Knife - Sword. The Grand Master announces, "Each contestant must choose four weapons to display your Ninjan skill and combat ability! Each weapon will have three rounds. (Pause) Black Eagle Contestants - select your weapons and inform your Elder." The eyes of the contestants scan across the Ninjans holding aloft the combat weapons. Some candidates share a quick huddle with their Elder. Jody looks up at the weapon choices, then turns to her Shoshone Elder. The man remarks, "Have you made your selection?" Jody nods and confidently replies, "Yes! I pick the Bow and Arrow, Open Hand, Spear - and the Sword." All the Elders lead their fighters to pre-assigned Tribal spots on the arena's perimeter. As the young contestants stay in their respective locations, their Elders leave and later return with their candidate's selected weapons.

## BEATING OF INDIAN DRUMS

The Black Eagle Judges assemble on their upper viewing level. A Tournament Referee walks to the middle of the arena to oversee each Combat Round. Jody and her fellow contenders stand at the perimeter and waited to be summoned. Jody glances about - some are cool and ready, while others are edgy and somewhat nervous. Jody inhales slow and steady - she lets out her breath and stands battle ready!

## BOW AND ARROW COMPETITION

Jody and five others stand with their weapon facing targets. The Referee lifts up his arm and the contestants fix arrow to bow. The Referee drops his arm to shoot. Jody pulls the drawstring of her black bow and fires - her arrow hits the bullseye dead centre! Three contestants miss the mark, and two strike the target. In another Round, a Tournament Official tosses a squash high into the air - Jody shoots and her arrow pierces it through. The others shoot their arrows - and miss. For the last Round, three lit candles are lined up straight - one arrow must extinguish all three flames. The contestants aim and shoot their arrows - only Jody's arrow puts out all three candles. The Referee extends his arm to Jody as the Winner!

## OPEN HAND COMBAT

In the first Battle Round, a young woman lunges and Jody grabs her and flips her over onto the arena floor. During the next Round, a big young guy throws punches at Jody, who ducks and blocks the attacks. She hits the attacker in a flurry of strikes and blows - that drops the guy to the ground. For the last Round, Jody fights an older man. He attacks with kicks and punches which Jody capably blocks and deflects, then Jody swiftly pivots with a powerful roundhouse that delivers a knockout! The Referee points to Jody - the Winner of Open Hand Combat.

## SPEAR

The contestants in this Competition throw traditional Indian Spears at swinging targets. Only Jody and two other participants hit their mark. For the second Round, the contestants - jab, swing and thrust spears in combat. Jody deflects a spear jab, twirls her spear shaft and strikes hard to disarm her attacker - she holds the spear tip at his neck - her opponent surrenders. In the last Round, A young man stands yards away confronting Jody, the two contestants lock eyes. Suddenly the opponent throws his spear at Jody with all his might - the spear flies directly at her. Jody quickly leans her body and catches the spear shaft. She stands victorious as she points both spears at her surprised opponent. The Referee smiles and extends his arm to Jody - the clear Winner!

## KATANA SWORD

There are six contestants with Katana Swords. The first Round has divided them into three pairs - each contestant must fight the other. Jody faces a young man who has apparent skill and quick moves. He and Jody spar with their Katanas. The young man swings and slices - his blade is fast. Jody blocks and counter-strikes. He swings hard and Jody ducks and unleashes a flurry of chops - her Katana blade moves swiftly. Jody strikes with blistering speed, her blade hits with ferocity, she out-manoeuvres and knocks her opponent's sword to the ground. From the other two pairs - a big guy and a young woman emerge as

Winners from their combat. The Referee points at Jody and the two other Winners. For the second Rounc, the Referee has the three Winners draw lots to determine battle order. Jody's lot is last, the big guy and the young woman must face each other. The big guy is strong and swings his Katana with power and might The young woman is very fast and agile. Each contestant shows skill and experience. The two battle and their swordplay is fierce - the man releases a big chop and the young woman twirls her blade to disarm her attacker. The big guy nods and yields defeat.

At this stage, the young woman and Jody face each other. By now, everyone's eyes are glued as the young woman and Jody circle each other, each with their steel blade ready. The girl swiftly thrusts her blade and Jody blocks. Jody swings and her female opponent deflects the attack. Their swordplay is fast with advanced technical skill. The girl lets out a barrage of chops and slices, Jody backs up to block, deflect and counter-swing. The girl stops to catch her breath. Jody seizes the moment and attacks with speed and force to release a torrent of thrusts, jabs, slices, and chops - the young girl is barely able to defend! The girl dives to her side, rolls on the ground and springs to her feet - ready for battle with her sword pointed at Jody. The two female warriors circle each other - their sword tips touch again and again. Jody glances around and notices the Black Eagle Judges, Tournament Ninjans, Tribal Elders, and all the Contestants are keenly watching. Jody takes a quick breath, then runs full out at her opponent - Jody swiftly swings her Katana blade left and right in rapid attack - the girl repeatedly blocks. Jody leaps and summmersaults over top the girl to attack from behind, her opponent turns to face Jody's flying blade - the young woman cannot keep up! Jody gives a powerful swing to knock the sword out of the young woman's hand. The female opponent stands empty-handed as Jody points the sword at her. The Referee walks to stand between the two and motions his hand to Jody as the **Champion**! Jody raises her eyes to the Grand Master and the Black Eagle Judges. The Officials smile their approval and bow - Jody bows respect in return.

## POUNDNG INDIAN DRUMS.  CHANTING

All the Tournament Contestants, Tribal Elders. Referees, Tournament Ninjans, are gathered on the arena floor before the Grand Master and the Black Eagle Judges. Only Jody stands alone in the space between the two groups. The Grand Master steps forward and proudly announces, "We honour you with this Tournament Scroll and the Black Eagle Sword. You are the Winner of this year's Black Eagle Tournament. - Congratulations Jody!" An Official awards the prized Trophies. Jody receives the Scroll and Black Eagle Sword with great humility and bows low in respect. (At this instant, she has a flashback to when Grandpa Carl taught her how to use the Katana sword). Jody looks at the Scroll and Black Eagle Sword with watery eyes. She turns about to the onlookers and lifts up the **Tournament Scroll** and **Black Eagle Sword** with a victorious smile. All the Contestants, Referees, Elders, and Tournament Ninjans show their support and CHEER!

# CHAPTER TWENTY-SIX
*The Wilderness Sunset!*

A Flight Attendant pushes a well stocked beverage cart down the passenger aisle. A few rows up, a hand motions to her. The Stewardess stops the trolly and looks at the Japanese man in sun glasses and business suit with his head bowed. The Flight Attendant politely asks, "Would you like something to drink?" The man lifts his head and nods. The Stewardess is briefly startled at the big scar that runs down his right cheek. The Japanese man responds in broken-English, "U-isuki. (Pause) Whiskey." The Flight Attendant smiles and sets out a short glass tumbler, puts in two ice cubes and pours the Whiskey. She hands him the tumbler full of Whiskey. He reaches up to hold the glass - a gold bracelet dangles from his wrist that features a small medallion with a snake!

It's mid afternoon as Karen sits in a Rehab wheelchair. Jody gently pushes her mom down the hall to the lounge seating area. She positions her mom and then sits down in an upholstered chair. Her mom remarks, "The doctors said your father woke up yesterday for a few minutes. (Excited) I can't wait to see him!" Jody comments, "I miss talking with him - I want to hear his voice again!" Karen reaches out to clasp her daughter's hand and mentions, "When we both get out of here - we'll celebrate your victory at Black Eagle! - Your Grandpa would have been so proud of you!" Jody gives a reassuring smile and adds, "When the Hospital releases you and dad - we can go to our favourite spot. It's been a long time since we were there last." Karen responds with a positive tone, "It'll be a real effort for your dad and I - but definitely worth it!" Jody smiles at her mom's comment.

**A FEW WEEKS LATER**

* * *

Karen, Brian and Jody stand on a smooth rock outcrop that juts out high above a beautiful wilderness valley. It's about to be a glorious sunset. Brian is still in recovery and weak, and Karen can only hobble with the aid of her aluminium crutch. Jody assists her dad and mom as the parents slowly shuffle forward a few paces for a better view. Brian feels inspired and remarks, "We've not been her since Jody was ten years old!" Jody chimes in a playful manner, "Tell me again - why this is your favourite place?" Karen puts her arm around Jody and Brian, and replies, "This was where your father asked me to marry him (Looks to Jody) And this was where we celebrated the news that I was pregnant with you!" Jody gives her parents a loving smile. The small family of three bask in the glowing sunset.

## BUSHES CRACKLE NEARBY

Suddenly - the Koroshi-ya steps out with his Katana sword raised - the steel blade gleams in the sunlight. The killer vehemently yells in broken-English, "Gaijin - American girl - you die!" Jody steps toward her assailant with an angry tone, "Go away! - Just leave me alone!" The professional killer lifts his sword high, sneers and threatens, "Stupid girl - easy to follow - Now, I kill - regain honour!" The man bolts at Jody and swings his sword. Jody leans to one side - the Katana blade slices open her clothing. Jody grabs and swiftly swings the metal crutch just in time to block the descending sword blade. **CLANG!** She forcefully spins the crutch to knock the blade away. The killer inches forward flailing the sword wildly. Jody holds the aluminium crutch as a weapon and backs up toward the lookout's edge. She glances down at the wilderness below. Brian and Karen, both incapacitated and too weak to help, anxiously watch. The Koroshi-ya creeps ahead cautiously. He sways the sword side to side to tease and scare. Jody inches backward and stops - she's close to the drop off. Brian yells, "Jody. Stop! - No further!" The assassin turns toward the parents a few yards away, then focuses on Jody and gloats, "After you dead - I kill parents!" Jody's adrenaline surges, her body tightens - she dashes at the killer with the crutch raised. The Koroshi-ya solidly plants his legs apart and swings the Katana with all his might! The steel blade slices directly at Jody's head. Jody ducks to slide through the man's legs, the blade swing cuts off part of Jody's long hair - the locks fall to the ground. Jody springs up and wields the metal crutch in a flurry of

122

blows - she strikes the man's head, sides, stomach, groin and face. Each blow sends the man backward - until the killer stands at the drop off. Bruised, beaten, bloody - the killer teeters back and forth at the edge. The man looses balance and starts to fall backwards with the Katana blade extended. Jody quickly grabs the sword blade to catch and hold the man from falling over. The sharp sword blade cuts into Jody's tight grip - blood oozes from her fingers. In pity, Jody looks into the man's desperate eyes - and pulls him to safety. Jody backs up. The man stands solid on the ledge, catches his breath and turns his head to look down at the valley floor far below. He looks at Jody, smiles sheepishly and bows. Jody slightly bows - still keeping her eyes on the man. The man's smile abruptly turns into a sneering scowl. He lifts his sword to attack - Jody quickly spins about with a powerful roundhouse that blasts the killer off the ledge - out into the air. The Koroshi-ya **SCREAMS** as he falls. Jody inches to the drop off and peers down at the killer's contorted dead body on the boulders and rocks below. She turns around and goes over to Brian and Karen and begins to help them up.

## ONE WEEK LATER

Jody kneels at her Grandfather's gravesite. She looks at the polished granite tombstone.

### KATHY LONG GRASS        CARL LONG GRASS

Jody reaches into her jeans and brings out the gold **SHOCHO TUKEN** - digs open a small hole and places the Ninja Token into the ground, covers it with dirt, then pats it down. Jody quietly whispers, "I love you Grandpa! You taught me everything I know - You're the one that deserves this great honour." Jody rises to her feet, gives her grandparent's tombstone a loving pat, then turns and walks away with a big smile. She pulls out her cell phone and touches the screen - KEI's PHOTO. Jody exits the cemetery and looks at the open road before her. High above in the clear blue sky, a black eagle soars with its wings spread out.

# CHAPTER TWENTY-SEVEN

*Somewhere in Japan*

The Beautiful Artist and the Bonsai Ninja step carefully along a narrow tunnel hewn from the hard rock. Their modern LED lamps illuminate the path as they move through the dark, further and further inside the mountain. The passageway was made long ago, when the Ninja Clan tunnelled deep into the mountain to create a secret chamber to store and hide their valuable treasure. Throughout their history, the Ninja Clan accumulated gold, diamonds, rare gems, silver, jade, and precious pearls. As the Beautiful Artist and the Ninjas shine their lamps - the light shows the large iron door and massive lock that guards and protects the chamber. The men move forward and gather beside the thick metal door.

The old Ninja Master remarks. "Shine more light." As more LEDS are focused where he stands, the elderly Ninja Master brings out the Golden Seal - and examines the base closely. He notices a Kanji that has a round dot - and presses. To the others' surprise, the bottom portion of the Golden Seal comes loose and sits in the Beautiful Artist's palm. The released item is a rectangular that is 2 inches in height. The indentations on each of the four sides are similar to the indentations of a key. The old man motions a nearby man to lower his lamp to cast more light on the massive lock. The old man looks at the unique piece in his hand - any one side could be the right key - the challenge and question is - which one? The legend passed down over time tells the danger of using the wrong key - the Chamber becomes destroyed forever! The Beautiful Artist studies the Kanji embellishments on the chamber door - one Kanji appears to stand out - that Kanji that can be written with three brush strokes. The aged Ninja Master examines the Key portion on all four sides - only one side has three indentations, the others sides have two, four and five indentations.

The men are both excited and nervous, everyone sensing the significance of the moment - standing at the very location of the Ninja legend and lore. The old man positions the Golden Key so the three indentations face the lock - he takes a breath and inserts the Key and turns. The lock over time has accumulated dust and debris and gives resistance. The Beautiful Artist exerts more pressure to turn the Key - the massive lock **CLINKS!** - the iron door cracks open. The old man steps back and motions for others to pry open the big door. As four men strain to pull the door open - dust and debris fall from the ceiling onto the group. As the dust settles - the iron door is wide open and the chamber inside is pitch black. The Beautiful Artist instructs, "Step inside and shine your lamps!" As everyone enters, the LED lamps reveal a vast chamber carved out of the mountain rock. The men shine their lights ahead - the old Ninja Master and all the Bonsai Ninja stare in awe - their mouths drop wide open. Light floods the interior making it sparkle, shine and glitter. Before them are piles full of gold, jewels, diamonds, jade, silver and pearls. The Beautiful Artist smiles with delight at finding the long lost **NINJA TREASURE!**

They all break out in CELEBRATION!

THE END

9 781777 310875